NOVELS BY

BALACHANDRA RAJAN

TOO LONG IN THE WEST   (1962)

THE DARK DANCER   (1958)

Too Long in The West

Balachandra Rajan

Too Long in the West

Atheneum : New York

1962

Contents

Too Long in The West

I

The Return of Sambasivan

Nobody could have known it was to happen.

Flying over the hills, one might have seen them lifting, layer upon layer, into a distance of blueness, the last blue an inversion of the sky itself. But down in the valley the lush dark green was dominant, the fronds and the splaying leaves hung over the road, dripping into its puddles, unhealthily, almost devouringly fertile. Behind there was a thickness and darkness, filtered through by strange noises and streaked only occasionally by the brilliant plumage of some startled bird. The road, euphemistically described as difficult to negotiate in wet weather, struggled and pushed its way through the jungle's embraces, persevering upwards, hoping for better things.

Then, for no reason that was clear, it ended. The forest stopped like the line of an ancient truce. The hillside broke free, first in gentle slopes, now green with cultivation, then with the curve of its ascent steepening but unbroken, thrusting up to the sandalwood-coloured house sprawled over its crest. The last rise was almost perpendicular, and the water fell over it in delicate ribbons that the morning sun made translucent, braided into a stream that curdled beside the road in its upper reaches, singing its way down till the forest claimed it. It was higher than one thought, groping up through the gloom and the demanding growth where the dampness was a hand laid on one's shoulder, sinking one into an identity with the dead leaves. Here the rain made the earth no more than fragrant. It was high enough to see the hills in their surrounding amphitheatre, dominated by the horn of Mahavir peak over which the monsoon clouds floated and were impaled. There was no competition to this eager upthrust. Elsewhere the contours against the sky were slackened, softened and smoothed away by many rains. Here only, the clouds' unending onslaught seemed to have laid bare an impenitence of the earth. It was not a high peak, and only in its last stages was it at all difficult by mountaineering standards. But to those unsophisticated by conquests elsewhere it remained an object of awe and desolation. Its shape was aloof, disturbing, satisfying. One found a challenge and then a repose in its loneliness.

Those on the hillsides would pause often to look at the peak, as they came home exhausted from the day's labour. The women would stand in the pose of temple sculptures, the inner line of the body straight and unbroken, the outer contour supply out-thrust, bearing the day's gatherings or the vivacious weight of a child. Familiarity never persuaded them to take the mountain for granted. They would watch the red disc of the sun glide into the emptiness beyond its summit and the darkness fall with an almost deadly suddenness as if it were crushing the day out of existence. Or they would watch it when the menacing forces of the monsoon were dominant and the clouds with their billowing purple belligerence rolled in procession over its adamant height. The clouds would close over it as well as the mists of legend. It was a wry story the hill told, mingling both reverence and laughter in ways that seemed inconsistent but which fitted the illusions of the mountain, cloud and mist. Perhaps it also enabled those telling it to live with more startling realities, with a world that was violent, both in its uprootings and in its benedictions, and which bloomed safely only in the oases of miracles.

Once, so the tale went, a holy man had sat on the summit of Mahavir mountain, facing the east in meditation for two years. By dint of austere and terrific penances he had succeeded in blending himself with the vegetation. The mountain goats played over him, unaware of his nature. Flowers sprang from his finger-nails and grass grew on his chest. On the second anniversary of his entrance into *Samadhi*, a snake chasing a lizard over the holy man's shin-bones missed his quarry and bit the saint's toe instead. Wrapped in contemplation, the *rishi* did not move; but the snake, intrigued by the unexpected taste of saintliness, took a second and even more poisonous bite. Thereupon the *rishi* wiggled his big toe and the snake turned immediately into a radiant young prince. He explained that three thousand and thirty years ago he had stumbled unwittingly over the foot of another less tolerant *rishi* on his impetuous way to a love tryst in the forest. The choleric sage had immediately reduced him to ashes with a single stare of his eye. Then, repenting somewhat, he had mixed the ashes with clay, con-

3

verting them into the world's second most poisonous snake. In this form, the unfortunate prince was condemned to slither all over Southern India till he discovered someone he could not kill with his bite. By wiggling his big toe the saint had now broken the spell and liberated the prince into his true essence.

The prince prostrated himself gratefully on the ground nine times, placed a garland in the presumed area of the saint's neck and, standing diligently on one leg, delivered a sermon on the delusions of *Maya*. At this moment, however, the *rishi*, wrapped in the recesses of his withdrawal, became dimly aware of certain mild disturbances in the penumbra of his meditations. Unconsciously he twitched the third finger of his left hand and because he had acquired great power through his penances this absent-minded gesture was enough to convert the young prince into a mango tree. Coming back into consciousness, the *rishi* became grievously aware of the mishap and since even his vast powers were unable to undo his own mistakes, he made such amends as he could by sitting under the tree in meditation for eight years. After this he expired peacefully and the tree absorbed his holiness.

This was the tale told by unemployed grandmothers, and when it was scoffed at by readers of modern fiction they were asked witheringly how else a mango tree could grow on the bare summit of Mahavir mountain. To this they had naturally no answer. The legend survived since it was never put to the test. No one was rash enough to climb the peak and therefore no one could seriously deny that the mangoes, eaten on certain auspicious Wednesdays, would bestow everything that the *rishi* had abandoned, including triumph in love, prosperity in marriage and success in examinations before the age of thirty. Indeed it was said that these gifts had been given once to two tramps, one blind and the other visionary, who were wandering in the vicinity of the mountain and on whose heads the mangoes fell after a fearful storm. They had long since left the neighbourhood. But the legend lived on and had not been disputed.

Today was Wednesday and an auspicious one. But there were neither square-shouldered young men nor virgins with new ear-rings and downcast almond eyes looking with trepidation and longing at the grim slopes and the remote, taunting fruit. Today was the day of a different benediction, superior and also more prosaic. It was the day for which all had waited, the day of recurrent good fortune, more tangible than any blessing born from the mountain's mists. It was in fact nothing less than the second Wednesday following the first new moon after the 29 April, which meant that it was the day of the annual miracle of Mudalur. All the two hundred and ninety-eight inhabitants of Mudalur were therefore in position where they should have been, on the felicitous road leading to the sandal-wood house. The women stood on the left side at two-hundred-foot intervals, their care-lined faces freshened with expectancy, hopefully erect, the hips unconsciously arched with the grace of those not too far from the jungle. The men lined the other side, spindle-shanked and bent-backed, dressed in a varied array of festive motley that contrasted bizarrely with their wives' plain but harmonious saris. Some wore only loincloths to make it apparent that their need was great. Others wore

5

home-spun shirts to imply that poverty could be borne with dignity. At the top of the incline Guruswami sported his top-hat, and the emaciated figure of Murugesan stood eerily in the athletic underwear which he had purloined from a bacchanalian Englishman in a thicket.

Their faces were bright because this was the true day of spring, inscribed not on the calendar but in the upsurging of life. It was the day when one's promises to frustration could be kept, when the lentils and rice could be sold and the child's slate purchased, when the skilled hands of the carpenter would no longer be idle. It was the day of prosperity, of the renaissance of Mudalur, when dreams could be exchanged and coconuts broken. It was the annual revival of the force that made the pineapples swell and the plantains weigh down the branches, that ripened the jackfruit and financed the marriages.

II

It was the day of Sambasivan's coming.

The cart jolted its way up through the mud and the heat, lurching over the boulders that the rain had denuded. The bullocks pulled at their burden rhythmically, resignedly, The crude heavy yoke had sunk into their shoulders till it seemed an extension of the unprotesting flesh. Behind them, the cart driver rhetorically cracked his whip and gave vent to a picturesque stream of adjectives. It flowed over the animals as the sun had and the rain would. They were not stirred by the expectancies of Mudalur, by the new life for which the people waited. Prosperity only meant that they would have heavier burdens to carry. They plodded on unvaryingly, unceasingly, as if nothing that ever changed would change around them, to the end of the tunnel and the relief of night.

Sambasivan sat at the rear, trying in difficult circumstances to look like a conquering emperor. His back was aching and his wife was beginning to scold him. A diadem of flies encircled his half-bald head. He peered forward hopefully along the road for the light that would first be an alien, tremulous vagueness and then focus suddenly as the end of the jungle. The contrast was no longer startling and spectacular to him as it would be to someone experiencing it for the first time. But, like poetry read often, it pleased him now with its justice. The end of the tunnel had to lead to a different world that was logical and entirely unexpected, that could not be predicted from the darkness or the earlier mountains between which one had passed. That was the trouble with most mountain railways. The valleys at both ends of the tunnel were too similar. They were two sides instead of being two worlds. One looked back and the hill under which one had passed was always too low to justify the suspenseful burrowing through it. It shut off nothing, exiled one from nothing. It was an obstacle instead of being a barrier. These were splendid thoughts, Sambasivan reflected, congratulating himself since his wife, Lakshmi, would not. He might even use them as the theme of his evening oration.

Lakshmi watched him with the apprehensions born of much experience. She could guess the depths of his enthusiasm from the colour of his ears, and looking at them now she saw no alternative to three miserable months in Mudalur. She shivered a little belligerently at the prospect. She had been brought up in a sensible town of one hundred and six thousand gossips and was therefore unable to find a valid reason for passing her holidays in the midst of jackals and yokels. Vacations were supposed to be spent with one's relatives so that one could sponge on them for at least three months in the year and save enough to dress reasonably on a professor's salary. But they did not even have any relatives in Mudalur. Nobody had, in fact, since all who could be sponged on had long since left, leaving Sambasivan as the sole source of largesse.

The sole source of largesse nodded his head and the motion made it obvious to Lakshmi that he was in the process of turning a well-turned thought. She found herself reflecting ruefully that he was not at all the person she had married. Her parents had chosen him for sound practical reasons – he talked less than anyone else and it was therefore to be presumed that he worked harder. In addition, two independent astrologers had singled him out as certain to achieve pre-eminence in his field. Discreet inquiries were made and there was no question of Sambasivan's talent in authoritatively answering examination questions. Marriage therefore seemed a prudent investment which would end satisfyingly with a position in the Indian Civil Service, a D.C.'s house with three butlers and two cooks, and sponging relatives whom Lakshmi could regally turn away.

The assumptions were correct but the inferences mistaken. Sambasivan worked hard, but consistently at the wrong things. He achieved pre-eminence, but in activities so lunatic that no one would have thought of competing against him. After dealing with all questions set in the past seventy years, he fell victim to a deplorable predilection for answering questions that no examiner ever asked. The bright expectations built on his future collapsed. His examination marks were revoltingly low. In the *viva voce* he questioned his interrogators. Finally when practising for his riding tests, his horse careered off on to an adjoining golf course, causing a high official to slice horribly into the rough.

Ignominy could not have been more complete and Sambasivan, in view of his overrated talents, was advised to abandon all hopes of the Civil Service and to concentrate modestly on inferior practices such as law and medicine. He did neither and took to crossword puzzles. His outraged parents now cut him indignantly off and even his wife, after tears and imprecations proved to be fruitless, was obliged to return to her family's capacious but reluctant bosom. Sambasivan continued on his obdurate course, eking out a tolerable living as a lecturer. After four years of perseverance he won the crossword puzzle prize of a famous periodical twice in succession, thereby becoming the first man to do so since the Emperor Asoka, who did not do it either.

He was now celebrated and even if the world did not beat a path to his door he could at least have joined the Cosmopolitan Club and acquired a partnership in a cinema or hotel. Instead, he had squandered all his unexpected and providential gains on this horrible sandalwood house so rightly called Hillview since nothing could be seen from it but depressing hills squashed by disgusting monsoons. It was not even a house in the normal sense, Lakshmi reflected angrily, what with a solar cooker on which no one had ever fried even a *brinjal* and a telescope protruding into the principal bedroom. And who had ever heard of a bathroom under a waterfall? It was all very well to argue as her husband did that the humiliations of the naked body required to be redeemed by the nobilities of nature, but her body was not as bad as that, she hoped, and if it was she would do better to keep it to herself.

For thirty-two years she had been dragging herself back to it, and what, she asked herself pointlessly, was the result of it all? An enormous misbegotten house which only a horde of dervishes could keep clean. Money poured down the drain like rotten rice to provide employment for a plague of louts and loafers. They could have had a place in the Nilgiris, growing eucalyptus trees and attending the Governor's receptions. All they had instead was this flea-bitten, weather-wasted dump to which even the postman only came twice a week. And as for the land – eighty-eight acres of unredeemed unkemptness, crawling with centipedes the size of fountain-pens and black ants as large as one's big toe. The jackfruit was rotten. The rice was fit only for rodents. The two rubber trees between them had not produced rubber enough to rub out even Gopal's spelling mistakes.

Gopal was growing up, slowly, hesitatingly. He would always be unready for the world he had fought to enter. Stubbornness held the shrinking shoulders erect, pushing him into an uncertain treacherous future in which perhaps the pity of different arms would claim him. And for Nalini, who inherited her hopes, the sacred fire would soon have to be lit, when she came back over the ocean to herself, to the promise of her eyes and the immemorial wisdom of her body. They were growing up and she could feel the difference isolating, ageing her, pushing her inevitably, dispassionately away into the society of gossips and grandmothers. Only in Mudalur there wasn't even the consolation of such a society. There were only the flames when the sunset touched the hill-tops and the encircling noises of the night and the emptiness opening in her heart when she sat in the big house as in a pit of loneliness. If she told that to Sambasivan he would refuse to understand. He wanted to be the great meaning, so he had said, with the ironic pompousness which she found in-furiating since it discounted all criticism in advance and enabled him to swallow all his own absurdities. He wanted to sit there dispensing charity, providing jobs, financing the existence of an entire village, making the difference between life and death. He wanted to be a tin god. It didn't matter if only the wilderness adored him.

She became aware of an invasion of light and of a cackling mounting on either side, which could have been applause or disguised derision. To Sambasivan it was an annual music. He looked upon his kingdom, the raised hands and joyful faces, the figures falling back on either side and a moderate feeling of elation claimed him. The measure of a man was what he did to others. And even the government with its vast resources, its brilliant brains and dedicated planners couldn't do what Sambasivan did every year in Mudalur. He was a pot-bellied, soft-hearted university professor who couldn't ride a horse or bully a bumpkin. But he mattered more than the forces of law and order. He mattered more even than the seasons and their fertility, the annual benediction of the rain on the spent earth. For the modest expenditure of six thousand rupees a summer, he had achieved superiority even to the elements.

He looked at his kingdom and considered it good.

The cart stopped and he dismounted. His legs had gone to sleep on the journey and he lurched a little before re-establishing the correct regal aplomb. Cascades of garlands were showered upon him. When he found it difficult to see between them he diverted them to the other members of his family.

A triumphal arch had been set up over the entrance. Above it were painted the words of a Sanskrit proverb declaring in effect that there was a mug born every minute. Sambasivan, who was ignorant of Sanskrit, walked under it believing it to be some sublime religious text.

The sun shone through a rift in the clouds, making it one of the rare occasions when one could read the sun-dial. It was two hours behind the actual time. Sambasivan's nephew had erred in his calculations and his uncle had immortalised the error in stone. If the whole family dined late as a result, that only served to demonstrate uncomfortably that mathematics had a practical value.

He walked into his house or rather the first of his houses. For the rooms in Hillview were not disposed according to any conventional plan. They were arranged concentrically in the manner of ancient cosmographies. To enlarge the house one merely added an orbit. The system had grown up in this way because it had been much too small in the first place and because Sambasivan refused to destroy what had already been erected. 'The point is to build and not to rebuild. India's poverty is too great for us to demolish its existing assets.' To Lakshmi's protests in the name of common sense, Sambasivan would deliver what he considered a crushing retort: 'You are not prepared to throw away even a rusty hairpin. How then can you expect me to throw away a building?'

So the house evolved organically, without a plan but with a history, as Sambasivan never tired of pointing out to those obliged to walk through five rings of bedrooms to the kitchen. Each new encirclement had to be lower than the last so that the windows of each room would admit the light and not simply the half-light of the room outside; as a consequence the house dribbled down a man-made slope, resembling nothing so much as a squashed pagoda. Sambasivan however was not deterred by the shape, or, if he was, he found more than adequate compensation in his ability to arrange the inhabitants of the house in a kind of moral hierarchy, determined by their distance from the centre. He had read Dante and such arrangements pleased him, particularly since by exiling those who had misbehaved to the outer circle of limbo he could imply reproof without inflicting discomfort. A house was a machine to live in, he would recall, and it should therefore contain a built-in ethical system. Sometimes he would try to demonstrate his impartial administration of this system by despatching himself to the fourth or even the fifth circle; but that, as Lakshmi pointed out, was usually when the roof of the first circle leaked. Sambasivan did not dispute this charge; he would only point out that the right deed was not less right because it was done for the wrong reasons.

Today he proceeded, as was his wont, to the interior. The assembled gathering was dispersed with a wave of his hand; they melted away without protest, knowing that he never held his durbars on the first day. On the first day he would contemplate his horizon, take stock of his resources, consider the administration of his estate.

In the inner sanctum he was alone. This was how he would have it and the room gave him no company. There was nothing in it except the telescope. He slept on the floor and in the morning rolled up his bedding. He prayed on a teak plank which, when he had used it, was pushed behind the roll. Once he had lined the circular walls with books, buying them recklessly and scanning them in haste. He was unable to turn the pages gently and every volume he went through was ravaged by his reading. He would underline and tick and dispute in the margins, tapping his high forehead, trying to feel the facts, scowling on under the feeble rays of the lamp, which he would not change because it had always been so. If he had time, it was a sin not to use it for acquiring knowledge. He continued to acquire it even when the knowledge was useless. Then the compulsion left him as a fever does and left him wondering how many other things he took for granted were fevers. He was not a philosopher, so he thought did not destroy him. He relegated the books to the second circle and looked at them often enough to save them from the mildew.

Then he lined the walls with pictures of gods and goddesses, Lakshmi, Saraswathi, Rama and the rest, in lotus-poised tranquillity or domestic contentment, but all of them pallid-coloured, bovine-faced, the four arms tacked on to them like some kitchen gadget. He relinquished them eventually, but not because they were bad art. It was simply that he no longer needed an image. He acquired no *Nataraja*, *Apsara* or *Yakshi*, no passionate bronze or stone swept by serenity, reaching into the world or thrusting beyond it. His mind did not grow; it merely shed a further layer of necessity. He prayed in the room, bareness reaching to bareness, perhaps because as the years washed one away there was nothing to come back to but the stripped husk. Yet he prayed with no sense of terror or repentance. It was a mild austerity and he ventured cautiously into it because it conferred a peace upon him which he did not thirst for but could drink when given.

Tomorrow he would be the jovial deity of the village. He would hector them, cajole them, devise unnecessary duties to employ them, be their pompous myopic effigy, unaware of the swindles going on at his elbow. He preferred to achieve his peace of mind in this manner, tangibly, keeping his fingers on the fruit, not by helping the beggar who immediately carried his misery to the next house, or by posting cheques to the institution beyond the reach of his heart. It was pleasant to be a momentary minor deity, however flawed and subject to hilarity. It was pleasant and it was not presumptuous, since in the wisdom of his country all but the greatest gods were less than *rishis*.

It rained the next morning as it usually did. The clouds drove over the hill-tops, blotting them out from memory. The front of the downpour moved onward, a sharply-marked line, the advance of a friendly army, leaving both liberation and ruin in its wake. Then it swept over and the whole world was part of the drenching, dissolving vagueness.

The marquee below the house was designed to collapse on every rainy morning. This meant that its rebuilding was a chronic problem on which Mudalur's manpower could be perennially employed. The thatched roof was already half-torn from its moorings. It flailed and flopped in the faces of the gathering who stood under it, patient and sodden in their umbrella hats.

Sambasivan sat under a brilliant circular awning which reminded one of summer in an Italian restaurant. An assistant held an umbrella over his head. At Sambasivan's right hand was a gilt mace which he used to keep order and to make him feel like *Bhima*. It was massive-looking but made of papier mâché. Twirling it gave him the sensation of vast strength but also reminded him from time to time that he could hurt no one with his imaginary prowess.

He flourished it now and the expectant whispering under the bobbing, circular hats subsided, leaving them inert like a forest of overgrown toadstools.

'The meeting is called to order,' said Sambasivan with dignity. 'The first item on the agenda will be to determine what the agenda is.'

Nobody knew what that meant, so everyone applauded.

'We will proceed,' said Sambasivan. 'Guruswami, the care-taker, will render his report.'

Guruswami stepped forward. The weather was too in-clement for his top hat and without it he felt slightly naked. He wiped his mouth on his shirt and rubbed his hands.

'Saar, I am a poor man, I have done my best.'

'Indeed he has,' somebody said ironically.

Guruswami ignored the interruption.

'I have done my best but it has been a bad year, O bringer of prosperity. The harvest was poor and the trees gave up no fruit. The land is accursed and a *Rakshasa* sleeps under it. The weeds flourish, saar, even while the paddy withers. And what the rats did not eat the thieves have stolen.'

'You're paid to stop thieving,' Sambasivan reminded him.

'Indeed that is my task, all-knowing guru, O giver of wisdom to the wise. But my legs are feeble and your estate is vast. The sun goes over it quicker than I go round it. I do my best, sahib, but I am only a mortal and wherever I am the thieves are somewhere else.'

'Enough of this nonsense,' said Sambasivan decisively. 'If you can't do what you're hired to do you're fired.'

The people tittered and Guruswami drew himself indig-nantly erect.

'Is this then to be my reward, O giver of bounty? For the long hours spent in the field? For the hard labour with which my back is broken? Are these my wages, O dispenser of justice?'

'You're fired,' Sambasivan repeated. He was pleased by his curt crisp tone which he told himself permitted of no argument. 'Apart from what you've sold there are at least ten maunds of stolen rice in your granary. And you've sent at least two cartfuls of my best fruits out of Mudalur.'

Guruswami spread his hands. They were empty and his whole posture suggested that it was obvious that the granary was emptier.

'It is impossible, saar. There can be no evidence for this monstrous accusation.'

'You've been doing it for six years,' Sambasivan pointed out. 'Nobody needs any evidence. But if you insist, we'll go along to your hut and find out exactly what the facts are. Only if they are as I say, you'll not only *be* fired but *stay* fired.'

Guruswami made his posture of wounded innocence even more dramatic.

'I will not protest,' he protested. 'When the great are cruel the poor must bear the affliction. I ask only that my children do not starve.'

'Nobody starves in Mudalur,' Sambasivan proclaimed like a minister making a statement for the press. There were murmurs of approbation which he acknowledged with a slight bow. 'My policy is one of full employment. Therefore though fired, you are also hired. Apply to my recruiting officer, Murugesan. He will engage you as a common labourer.'

'A labourer, saar? I, saar, who have served tea to eminent Englishmen?'

'A labourer can be caretaker if he works hard enough.' It was a fine democratic precept, Sambasivan thought, and there was a rhythm of justice in its application. Each summer Guruswami rose through devoted work. Each winter he fell through negligence and the corruption of power. His recurring fate reflected larger mysteries such as Nemesis, hubris and the chain of *Karma*.

Guruswami responded, florid as ever, immersed in his own fortunes, chanting his hopes as if he had never before sung them. Yet his extravagance was not lacking in a certain note of irony. The respect in his voice was genuine; but there was a tincture of amusement also.

'I take hope, O avatar of justice, upholder of the law and of the lotus. May the heavens rain their benefactions upon you.'

'It's raining,' observed Sambasivan, 'but not, I'm afraid, with blessings.'

The gathering chuckled dutifully at his humour.

'Next case, please,' said Sambasivan, tapping his mace.

'My groins ache, and I shiver in the fields, sahib.'

He was an emaciated man, almost ghostly, the flesh so far consumed that the veins on his hands stood out in blue ridges. Sambasivan forced himself to look at him, feeling the tremor in his spine which was largely distaste but which contained an incipience of fear also. He had seldom been ill and therefore flinched from illness. He had to remind himself that those who suffered from it had only rarely brought it upon themselves.

'You've no business to be in the fields, my friend,' he said awkwardly. 'Stay in bed and use the medicine which I gave you.'

'My sons have left, sahib.' He said it without rancour. Old age was supposed to be protected but the realities were different from the gospel. To be abandoned by those who could look after one was the beginning of the invasion of darkness, the first wave in the washing away of life.

'Sahib, there is no one but I to do the work.'

'Be assured that the work will be done.' It should have been pronounced as a benediction, but it came out instead a small-voiced admission of the fact, grudging, inadequate, a reassurance to him who gave, rather than an alleviation of the need it confronted.

'Sahib, you are generous, very generous.' The old man's voice was throbbing with his tears. 'I pray to the goddess of the earth to bless you.'

'Next case,' said Sambasivan, clearing his throat uncomfortably.

It was Kesavan, the carpenter. 'What is your pleasure for me this summer, sahib? What work of craftsmanship can I perform for your delight?'

'For heaven's sake, don't make another almirah.'

'I can make a chest-of-drawers, sahib.'

'There are eighteen of them already.'

'Let him carve a statue of Guruswami,' someone suggested.

'Good idea,' said a wit at the back. 'On a dark night it'll frighten away the thieves.'

'I see it,' cried Kesavan, his face suddenly lighting up. 'Inspiration has seized me,' he added more poetically. 'Sahib, I shall make your revered wife a dressing-table.'

He saw Sambasivan's face fall and hastened to elaborate.

'Truly I know, sahib, that there are already six of them. But this is a table such as not even Delhi has seen, at which Radha herself might perform her sylvan toilet. It will consist of an egg supporting an elephant, supporting a tortoise on which there will recline the great snake *Sesha*, with a mirror on his head and four drawers of inlaid rosewood on his tail. Sahib, the whole world has never seen anything like it.'

'I'm quite sure that it hasn't.' Sambasivan hoped that his lack of enthusiasm was evident. In these moods the carpenter was a difficult man to deter.

'Has my humble self your permission to proceed?'

'Proceed, by all means,' said Sambasivan resignedly. 'It'll feed your family and keep you from the arrack.'

'Saar, I need forty rupees for the rosewood.'

The look in his eyes made it clear that the money was likely to be put to less serious uses.

'Apply to my treasury officer, Murugesan,' said Sambasivan. He knew he had guessed correctly from the man's crestfallen expression. 'Murugesan will accompany you to make sure that the rosewood is bought.'

He decided to speed up the proceedings.

'The ladies will make sweets for all the people of Mudalur. The water-diviner will look for a new well. When he has found one the mason will build an ornamental pond next to it. The strong young men of the village can pull up the weeds which Guruswami has neglected. Those who still lack work can once again dredge the swamp at the foot of the rubber trees. For the specially diligent there is a special task. The eight new acres I bought last year are to be cleared at one and a half times the usual rates. Higher rewards will be paid in future for poisonous snakes killed – six annas for ordinaries, ten for Russell's vipers and fourteen for a cobra. But anyone bringing in a grass snake will be fined a rupee.'

He paused to make sure that his plan of action had been understood.

'Any comments or questions?' he asked finally.

'Down with him,' said a clear belligerent voice.

There was a scandalised rustle in the gathering. The umbrella hats pirouetted as the heads beneath them turned to the source of the voice. Sambasivan was so surprised that he forgot the menacing flourish of his mace which would have been the right way of restoring order.

The young man swept off his hat so that everyone could see him. He held it in front of him as if it were a shield. He had square shoulders, clear-cut features, intense eyes and a chest which was ready for the arrows.

'Down with him,' he repeated. 'Can't you see that he only wants to exploit you?'

The gathering did not see it, but the young man's confident tone made them begin to wonder if they were lacking in perceptiveness.

'Exploit!' spluttered Sambasivan. He would have preferred to be icy but his emotions were boiling. 'Exploit! Just look at the money I spend. And do I make a quarter-anna out of it? Ask Murugesan, he keeps my accounts. He'll tell you that I run this place at a loss.'

'Of course you do,' the young man retorted smugly. 'Everyone runs at a loss. All the railways and all the bus corporations. And the British ran India at a terrible loss too.'

'Maybe young Raman's right,' said someone doubtfully.

'If we're running at a loss we must be paying for it somewhere.'

'Nobody ever does anything for nothing.'

'It's our children who'll probably have to suffer.'

'He's bartering our lives without even consulting us.'

'What's wrong with Mudalur, anyway? Why can't he make a decent profit out of us?'

'He isn't God,' the young man shouted, accusingly pointing at Sambasivan as if he were the devil incarnate. 'Why must we build these worthless monuments for him? That's all that he ever thinks about – his never-ending, flabby, pot-bellied, navel-worshipping vanity. Another ring around his monstrous house. A useless pond next to an unwanted well. Why won't he let us do something for ourselves? Why can't we make something from which *we* can benefit?'

'Well said, young Raman.'

'That's the trouble with us Indians.'

'Holding our hands out like beggars.'

'Always pouring ghee into someone else's rice.'

'No question about it. He's a – whatever that long word is.'

'I got this ague, working for him in the swamps. Now he gives me medicine like an act of charity. He tells me I am to stay at home. Where else am I to stay, thanks to him, the scoundrel?'

'Down with him. We'll run him out of Mudalur on a donkey's back.'

'Let's burn his shambling, rambling house. It's always been a blot on the landscape anyway.'

Sambasivan sat there unable to control the tumult. He wanted to be masterful, to silence them aloofly with the power of his personality. He would have liked to stand up, icily contemptuous, the authority cracking in his voice like a whip, his mesmerising eyes boring like gimlets, individually,

into each member of his audience. He had always basked in
Walter Mitty day-dreams and the Mudalur house was an
effort to make fantasy real. Now the crisis was upon him and
he wasn't even a tenth of what it required. He squirmed
dejectedly and shuffled his feet. He was beginning to feel as
flimsy as his mace.

'If you burn down my house,' he said in a small voice
which to his surprise was reasonably steady, 'I'm not going
to pay you to rebuild it.'

'Won't pay us, eh!'

'Absolutely unreasonable.'

'How the devil does he expect us to earn a living?'

'Just a minute,' cried Kesavan, scratching his head. The
wheels in his head were beginning to turn and were adding
up to a disconcerting total. 'Just a minute, if you please.
There's something funny going wrong in all this. I've got
four months' drink locked up in that dressing-table. I'm not
spilling it all just to burn down a house.'

Sambasivan stood up and swallowed a mouthful of
courage.

'I shall not stay if I am no longer wanted. The ninety-
seven people I employ each summer can always find some
other means of work.'

Several of the ninety-seven began to look disturbed.

'Don't listen to him,' cried Raman. 'You can always help
yourselves. You can live with dignity on the fruits of your
labour. And it'll be real work in a common partnership. Not
slaving for him, building his ugly dreams.'

'Burn my house if you care to,' said Sambasivan airily. He
was feeling much more like his fantasy now. 'Then you can

sit and smoke *beedees* in the rains. That is, if the monsoon doesn't put them out. And if your wives are able to sell their charms for *beedees*.'

'Saar, we implore you to stay.'

'Do not abandon us, O fountain of benevolence!'

'I am grievously offended,' Sambasivan continued. 'For many years I have ruled over you as a father. I have let no man be idle, however meagre his gifts. When work could not be found I have brilliantly invented it. I have looked after the sick, I have assisted the weak. Must the clear stream of my charity be fouled by the scum of your insults?'

'We'll produce twice as much,' the young man shouted. 'We'll work twenty hours a day. We'll build a granary of stone and pile it high. Then with what the food buys we'll build a school for our children.'

'Twenty hours a day. I've never worked more than five and a half in my life.'

'Who's the slave-driver, I ask you?'

'A school indeed! Not for me. Not if it's going to produce more Ramans.'

'Let's throw him in the swamp.'

'Let's run him out of Mudalur.'

They advanced upon Raman, who threw away his shield and bared his breast.

'Kill me, if you want to,' he declared intimidatingly.

'We aren't going to kill you,' Kesavan pointed out. 'We're going to give you a mud bath.'

Raman began to look perturbed. It was hardly a suitable punishment for a marytr.

Sambasivan intervened.

'One moment, my friends,' he said blandly. 'Let us not resort to violence, however provoked. As the poet says, mercy must season justice.'

The people scratched their heads. They couldn't recall which particular poet had said that. And it didn't seem a particularly sensible thing to say. It would have been far more interesting to tar and feather Raman.

But it was best to comply with Sambasivan's wishes.

They stepped back from Raman and he stalked away angrily from them.

'You're a pack of fools,' he told them, when he had reached the edge of the marquee. 'You're a collection of cows listening to what you think is Krishna's flute. If the food was taken right out of your mouths you'd sing a song about the pleasures of fasting.'

'He's energetic with his opinions,' Sambasivan commented. 'Let's see if he's equally energetic with his hands.'

'Splendid idea!'

'We'll make him work in the swamp.'

'Twenty hours a day, like he's always advising us.'

'And if he doesn't fall in of weariness we can push him in anyway.'

'Audience dismissed,' said Sambasivan smugly.

They went down the hillside, picking their way amid the puddles and rivulets, the wet clothes clinging to the skimpy bodies, elated and dancing in the mist of the rain.

'Did anything happen?' Lakshmi asked, without interest. She had squeezed a blackhead out of her nose, which she considered a far more satisfying accomplishment than the decisions taken at these pompous durbars.

'A few things,' said Sambasivan offhandedly. 'There was a little trouble, to tell the truth, but I disposed of it in my usual decisive fashion.'

'Trouble,' grumbled Lakshmi. 'As if we haven't enough of it.'

It was not a proposition her husband wanted to dispute. There was obviously a burden on his wife's heart, so he waited dutifully to have it laid on his shoulder.

'Just look at the mess we're making of Nalini's marriage.'

The *we* was broadminded, since, as far as Lakshmi was concerned, there could have been no question where the blame lay.

'But she isn't married,' Sambasivan objected.

'That's just the trouble,' she wailed. 'Who'll ever marry her with an American university education?'

'Oh I don't know, you know. I've known it happen.'

'A woman's place is in the kitchen,' Lakshmi said flatly.

'How edifying, my dear! I didn't realise you'd moved the dressing-table in there.'

'Yes, be funny,' she scolded. 'But marriage is no joke.'

'I see no obstacles,' Sambasivan declared. He was falling into his professorial mood and the words came forward dignified and self-conscious, as if they had all taken university degrees. 'She is endowed with beauty, modesty and wit, to which education has been dexterously added. Such a combination can very well speak for itself. But to make it speak louder we have proclaimed it in every leading journal.'

'That's just it,' she said. 'Advertising. Oh Sivan, Sivan, why did you have to do it? Anyone would think we were getting desperate.'

'What's wrong with advertising? The Government does it when they want to buy a steel-mill.'

'They'll think she's ugly as sin.'

'That isn't what I said, dear. May I remind you of my well-chosen text?'

He took the frayed piece of paper out of his pocket, reading the words as if they were buttered rice on his tongue.

' "*Vadama* girl, educated yet domesticated. Fair of face, ravishing of form. Unprecedented paragon will marry whoever deserves her." '

'There you are,' he said proudly. 'Perfection in a nutshell.'

'Even I don't believe it,' said Lakshmi. 'And if I don't, what makes you think that anybody else will? I'll tell you what they'll think. They'll think she's ugly and that her mother's venomous. They'll think you're a profligate who can't afford a dowry. They'll think we're both idiots and *you* probably are one.'

'*Toujours la politesse,*' said Sambasivan feebly. It was the only French that he knew.

'Don't think,' Lakshmi blazed at him, 'that you can escape from the truth by speaking a foreign language. I'll tell you what you've done. You've ruined my only daughter's marriage prospects. You've corrupted her maiden virtues with education. And home-made corruption isn't good enough for you. Oh, no! You have to send her to Columbia. That means she's superior to everybody else. She'll be priggish and insufferable. She'll be too big for her shoes and too swanky for her sari. And even if she isn't everyone will think so.'

'You think too much, I'm afraid,' said Sambasivan, 'about what other people are going to think. Kindly permit them to draw their own conclusions. And there is no question of Nalini not doing what she is required to. She has been given the best possible education only to equip her to perform her wifely duties. She will now perform them with an efficiency that justifies my considerable expenditure. I shall choose a young man with the correct sense of proportion in these matters.'

'She'll never fit in,' Lakshmi prophesied dismally. 'She's been too long in the West. She's forgotten our language and will turn up her nose at our food. She'll want to bathe with soap instead of *sheyaka* powder and to clean her teeth with toothpaste instead of a *neem* twig. And worst of all she'll talk back to her husband.'

Her last remark tempted Sambasivan sorely but he thought it best to reply in a less sensitive area.

'I can't understand all this fuss about toothpaste,' he said blandly. 'I seem to remember that you use cold cream. Perhaps you'll tell me it's a Vedic invention.'

'I belong to the older generation,' she retorted, 'and so I can afford to indulge in such things. It's a frivolity in me. In her, it's a rebellion.'

She realised that she was being diverted from the main stream of her complaints.

'Very well, let's assume that America has done her no harm, and that other people don't think so. It isn't true, but let's assume it is. But that's only the beginning of our troubles. You've read only one half of your silly advertisement. And what does the other half say? "Apply in person to Hillview, Mudalur." Mudalur, mind you. Not to Madras or Madura or even Kodaikanal, but to a flea-bitten, fraud-infested pigsty of a place, which isn't on any map and which only a lunatic could find. Do you seriously expect anyone in his right mind to come here? In the middle of the monsoon? Up a road that's no better than a river of mud?'

'Perhaps the going is a little rough,' Sambasivan admitted. 'But nothing venture, nothing win, you know. None but the bold deserve the fair and all that.'

'Only a fool would be fool enough to come here. And I'm not giving my only daughter to a fool. If she must be married I want it to be done sensibly, in a proper house, with all the would-be husbands driving up in cars and neighbours around knowing exactly what's happening. Not here, where even the postman couldn't care less.'

The corners of her mouth were beginning to tremble. She fumbled indignantly for her handkerchief, at the waist of her sari.

There was a knock at the door, to his relief. He had never been good at consoling tearful ladies and, realising that, he would have asserted his authority with unnecessary heaviness. He didn't want to hurt her, but he would have probably done so to defend himself.

The young man came in like a calamity out of the rain. He had an umbrella, but the wind had broken its ribs. It flapped despondently and dripped water into his collar. He took his spectacles off, mistook the Kashmiri carpet for the doormat and walked with Groucho Marx strides to the nearest armchair in the seventh circle. He sat down and twirled his umbrella vigorously, drenching Sambasivan who had incautiously approached him. Then he put his left ankle on his right knee, blew unnecessarily on his glasses and wiped them on the turn-ups of his trousers. He put them back on a remarkably large nose. His eyes had a look of perpetual surprise in them at being able to see round so enormous an obstacle.

He looked around the room, as if it were an undesirable legacy.

'Interesting house,' he observed eventually. 'Was it Courvoisier or Corbusier who designed it?'

'Oh, it wasn't designed,' Sambasivan explained. 'It just happened. Rather like the English constitution.'

The young man frowned at him, making him realise that the British were no longer a model.

'I am not impressed. Everything must be planned. In my scheme of things nothing can be permitted to happen.'

'This is *our* house incidentally,' Sambasivan said.

'Quite so. That is precisely why it concerns me. Now will you be good enough to show me car?'

'Car!' exclaimed Sambasivan, mildly flabbergasted. 'What car? You can see for yourself there isn't even a garage here.'

'You are unable even to afford a car?'

'Of course we can and do. But no one could possibly drive a car to Mudalur.'

'The point is validly taken,' admitted the young man. 'In

31

that case you may show me car insurance policy.'

'What business is it of yours?' Sambasivan exploded.

'Everything that involves you happens to be my business.'

Sambasivan controlled himself. He reflected a little. A flicker of recognition come into his eyes.

'I see,' he said. 'I am beginning to understand. You are presumably an income tax collector.'

'My name is Satyamurti.'

'We are delighted to meet you.'

'But I represent nobody but myself.'

'In that case you are an impertinent scoundrel. Get out of here before I throw you out.'

'Get out of here!' the young man echoed indignantly. 'I've come here only at your request.'

'My request!' exclaimed Sambasivan, amazed.

'You are P. S. Sambasivan, are you not? This is Hillview, Mudalur, is it not?'

They were both facts which nobody felt inclined to dispute.

'You are author of advertisement in *Hindu* of fourteenth ultimo? Indicating availability of daughter, presumably virgin?'

'Yes, indeed,' said Sambasivan, the light beginning to dawn.

'I have come in response to aforesaid offer. Kindly indicate where I may inspect said bride.'

'I am afraid you can't see her,' Sambasivan apologised.

'She is betrothed already? Surely not? I have come post-haste and with the utmost dispatch.'

'But *she* hasn't, you see. She's still on her way from America.'

'America?' inquired Satyamurti sharply. 'Said bride has been in America? She has bathed every day, I trust? She has not touched fish, flesh, fowl or any concoction containing yolk of egg?'

'She has behaved,' said Sambasivan, 'exactly as the daughter of her father should.'

The young man peered at him dubiously.

'Very well, I will not pre-judge. Nevertheless may I please see suitable photograph?'

'Yes, of course, of course,' said Lakshmi eagerly. She wasn't particularly taken by the young man, but she relished the thought of letting him see what was evidently too good for him.

She went to her dressing-table and rummaged in her collection, picking out the one she had always liked most. It was Nalini in half-profile, the angle setting off the clear-cut lines of her face, too serious to be pretty, too delicate to be handsome. Her mouth was pensive, but was saved from the Indian sadness by eyes which were deep-hued and brilliant and which even in repose were almost vivacious. She looked out of the picture with a faint demureness as if nothing else existed but the person who looked back at her and from whom in her modesty she looked slightly away.

Lakshmi took it up, feeling a slight pang of regret. She was beautiful and if one hadn't lived with her beauty from the beginning it wasn't right that one should eavesdrop on it.

But after some hesitation she gave Satyamurti the picture.

He got out of his chair and stood directly under the hurricane lamp. He held the picture close to his eyes and perused it diligently, seeming to move his nose along its length and width. But while his gestures were comical there was also a magisterial air about him which made Lakshmi hold her breath in alarm, wondering how many times he had gone through this performance.

He put it down eventually, and cleared his throat.

'Face seems entirely satisfactory,' he announced. 'Question is, however, what is behind and under the face?'

'It's about time *we* asked you some questions,' said Sambasivan grimly.

The young man bristled a little.

'Ask any question you want. My name is Satyamurti, meaning truth-teller.'

'And what is your home town?' asked Lakshmi.

'I come from Kumbakonam.'

Lakshmi went off into a peal of laughter. The young man had expected it. He shrugged his shoulders and looked at her contemptuously.

'I am sorry for you if you listen to stupid *canards*.'

'Don't take it amiss,' said Sambasivan adroitly. 'It is not you but the story that she's laughing at. We all know the facts, of course; that there are no more liars in Kumbakonam than anywhere else.'

'And what do your parents do?' Lakshmi continued.

'My mother and father both are long since dead.'

He said it remotely as if the fact itself were too dead to disturb him. But there was a reproof in his tone which made Sambasivan apologise.

'I am extremely sorry. We didn't mean to hurt you.'

'Of course, of course,' Lakshmi agreed with a slight hint of impatience. 'But, if I'm not being too inquisitive, what

34

were your mother and father before they –'

Her right hand described a tactful semicircle.

'I don't know,' said Satyamurti unhappily. His eyes were moving down a much-trodden road.

'You were too young even to know that? But surely one of your relatives must have told you?'

'I don't know who my mother and father were.'

His mouth set in a straight line and he squared his shoulders.

Lakshmi leapt out of her chair, her fists clenched, her eyes blazing.

'You dare to come here knowing you don't know that! An orphan, a foundling, the son of a slut and a sod. You dare to enter a respectable house! This is what the advertisement has done. This is the sort of person that comes to Mudalur. Mongrels and curs solicit the hand of my daughter.'

Satyamurti walked again under the light, patient, erect, a blind man trying to see. He flinched from each word very slightly and almost automatically. The foreknowledge of pain could never make the pain less.

'Judge me by what I do,' he said at last.

He was not demanding anything or even defending himself. He stated it simply as a right which could not be given.

'I don't care what you do,' screamed Lakshmi. 'Do what you want, I don't care what you do. But get out of here and do it somewhere else.'

'I am penniless scholar,' the young man said. 'I scrub floors in order to buy books. I read by night under the light of street-lamps. Judge me by what I do. In no examination has any student beaten me.'

His earlier aggressiveness was exposed now. It was his way of seizing the initiative, of keeping away from the truth. Now the truth was out and he was once more against it, against the wall where the hunt always ended. He stood his ground since there was nothing else he could do. It was useless to be defiant, undignified to shout back. He stood there waiting for the next adversity, squaring his shoulders with a touching pride.

Sambasivan hummed and hawed and looked out of the corner of his eye at Lakshmi. He tried to screw up his courage into decency.

'You've come a long way,' he said eventually. 'And in bad weather too. There's no harm in your staying here for a few days.'

'Stay here!' cried Lakshmi. 'Have you gone out of your mind? We don't even know who he is. How do you know he isn't a dacoit? How do you know he won't strangle us in the night and make off with the little we possess?'

'I am my father's son,' the young man said, giving back the words deliberately to their author.

Sambasivan winced in acknowledgement. But Lakshmi's memory was conveniently short.

'Much help that is when we don't know your father. You've no business, no right whatever to be here. If it's too late for the train out of Arkayam, which it isn't, get out of here and sleep in the servants' godown.'

'Silence, woman!' Sambasivan thundered unexpectedly. It was very seldom indeed that he spoke to Lakshmi in that way. In fact he was so taken aback by his own sternness that he himself did not know quite what to do next.

'He's soaked to the skin,' he said, after some hesitation. 'Can't you see that his teeth are chattering? We don't want the poor fellow catching pneumonia. Go into the kitchen and have some *rasam* made for him.'

Lakshmi obeyed, but gave him a venomous look.

'*Rasam*, indeed!' she grumbled. 'If only I could make it hot enough. But even if I threw in all the chillies in India it still wouldn't be as stinging as I'd want it.'

'Don't mind her,' said Sambasivan, as she stalked into the kitchen. 'She doesn't really dislike you. It's just that she's very fond of her daughter.'

'Thank you for your kindness, sir,' the young man said awkwardly. 'It's the first time I haven't been thrown out.'

'You've done this before, then?' Sambasivan inquired.

The young man nodded his head.

'How on earth do you manage to pay for the train fares?'

'I don't travel by train,' said Satyamurti. 'I have a bicycle,' he added rather proudly.

He saw the expression on Sambasivan's face.

'Well, it isn't really very much of a bicycle. There was a judge's son and I helped him in maths. It was six years old and so he let me have it.'

'I wasn't thinking of that,' Sambasivan explained. 'I was thinking that it's three hundred miles to Kumbakonam.'

'I have come longer distances.'

'What for? What's the sense of it? Why come all that way simply to get your face slapped?'

'You cannot understand,' the young man said. 'You can never have felt the loneliness. Sometimes I cycle under the peace of the night sky, and the plains stretch endlessly out

37

as far as one can remember or imagine. There should be a home for everyone in that vastness. But not for myself. Then I feel the desperation. Perhaps those who write advertisements are a little desperate also. Perhaps it is possible for two desperations to join.'

He flushed a little. 'I am troubling you with trifles. I shall go out and bring in my belongings.'

When he left, Lakshmi, who had been going slow with the *rasam*, reappeared. She put her hands on her hips and turned the corners of her mouth down in the classic posture of an upbraiding wife.

'Yes, I know, I know,' said Sambasivan hastily. 'I've been making an ass of myself.'

'An ass is the epitome of intelligence compared to you.'

'The trouble with you is that you've no sense of pity.'

'The trouble with you is that pity is the only sense you have. You're sorry for all the swindlers and leeches of Mudalur. Your heart bleeds for every orphan that stumbles out of the storm. You want to be everyone's husband but your wife's, and the father of everyone except your daughter.'

'Let's give him a fair trial,' Sambasivan appealed to her. 'He was the first to answer. We shouldn't turn away the first of many blessings.'

'He's an evil omen,' said Lakshmi.

'If he's truly evil we should placate him with *rasam*.'

Lakshmi smiled a little. She couldn't be angry for long. She spread out her arms in a vast and flamboyant gesture of forgiveness.

'It is my *karma* to have to put up with your foolishness.'

'It is mine,' he retorted, 'to have to be wedded to your arguing.'

She had to restrain herself from demonstrating the truth of his remark.

'No great harm's done, anyway,' she concluded. 'After all, Nalini *is* her mother's daughter. And since she's that, she cannot possibly choose him.'

Sambasivan said nothing, but the thought flashed through his mind that the teller of sad truths from Kumbakonam might in the end be worthier than the rest.

2

Nalini

I

THE TRAIN stopped at the station as if it were a love tryst. Its onward progress was an expedition and its late arrival always an event. Sellers of sweetmeats and vendors of bananas and cooks with hot Indian meals wrapped up in luscious leaves scuttled up and down the curious length of the carriages, each of them emitting his characteristic cry. Here and there a beggar thrust a wailing arm into a window and faces grown suddenly hard were swiftly averted.

In the European-style restaurant a man sat munching a rissole and washing it down with anæmic orange squash. Being the proprietor, he was compelled to undergo this penance in order to demonstrate the charms of his cuisine. Nobody was convinced by the demonstration. He wasn't himself, and his nose sniffed longingly at the real food outside. Two years ago he would have been reasonably busy, with lobster-faced Englishmen and their pimply offspring, and Indians strutting in, throwing their flyweights around, screaming invective at the punkah-wallah, lunching on stale fried fish, tinned fruit salad and coffee, with ideal milk, while the fruit ripened temptingly on the trees outside. Now the British had gone, business had collapsed, and the mimics had all found a different image to parody.

Nalini's carriage was opposite the restaurant. It was reserved for ladies and, as no other lady had the temerity to travel unescorted, she had the entire four-berthed compartment to herself. She could thread her way back into the past, undisturbed. It swept up against the windows arid and immediate, as the train thudded across the dust-drenched plains and shrieked warningly towards the foot-hills of remembrance. So little had changed. The stunted trees were still there to the last leaf; the monkeys still scampered over the striated rock which reared out of the earth, imprisoning a prince's dead pride. She could never have left this world – the flat, baked, red earth, windless and eventless and endless, and the hills hazing out of it, suddenly real with a coolness that one could taste. And yet she had left it three years ago. She remembered the farewells and the garlands, the admonitions and the trembling last-minute advice, the sea-sickness pills and the case of herbal remedies to guard her against various foreign subversions. Her mother had been in tears because the day was not auspicious and the P. & O. captain had refused to postpone the sailing. She had promised everyone to be good and had meant it, because she was a little frightened and lonely, as the arms held out to her were sucked away and the horizon swallowed up the curve of the past. It was strange to be on a real ocean, instead of on that comforting ocean of land through which the trees broke and on which the villages were anchored and which she knew that the hills must always end. The propeller throbbed under her, drilling into the distance, to an unknown future of postcards and prospectuses, and she paced up and down as the night softened the sigh of the water and the stars shone consolingly and unchangeably over the unending wedge of the ship's wake.

Despite her misgivings, she was entranced by her cabin. It was the first room that she had ever had to herself. Standing in the middle, she could touch all the four walls; it gave her a feeling of solidity as well as of liberation. She hung a picture of Saraswati at the head of her bed and prayed devoutly to the goddess every night because she was going abroad to be educated, and though she intended to enjoy herself she wanted also to be true to the family's dreams. There were stars in her eyes soon as well as outside the port-holes; she became confident that the ship was moving towards a meaning.

Main Deck adopted her as one of its treasures. She won competitions, patiently answered every question about India and learned to dance with a feeling of giddy sinfulness which she rectified by praying to the goddess of proportion. She experienced everything with an intense innocence, but the enthusiasms flowed into a mind already fashioned into the severe silhouette of the family ideal. Therefore while wide-eyed she was also clear-eyed. She grew with whatever happened to her; she was vivid and grave, vivacious and withdrawn, alive to her finger-tips yet with a self-contained calm in the centre of all that she did. She did not find the new world; rather it discovered her, unlocking the qualities she had always possessed.

And the new world was new. It lay across two continents

and three oceans. It was the difference between being herself and the compromised product of her family's pushes
and pulls. It was having her own cabin. It was to be able
to walk around the stern of the ship and count the stars
without naming the constellations. The new world found
her long before the half-way house of England's chalk cliffs,
before the friendly blue of the Mediterranean had given
place to the impersonal grey of the Atlantic. If even the
ocean was different, she promised herself, it meant there
was more to be learnt on the other side. When the second
ship set its course across the waters she was already the
citizen of the future into which it plunged.

The last night was cold and foggy and, lacking winter
clothes, she shivered and pouted, wondering what enigma
would reveal itself in the mists. But the morning dawned
clear-cut as a travel advertisement. She breathed the air
with hopeful satisfaction; it smelled infectiously of diesel
oil and prosperity. The ship nosed up the harbour towards
the benediction of the statue. There were islands in the sun
wherever she looked, surrounded by revolving rings of
automobiles, scurrying endlessly into tunnels and bridges.
The fingers of Wall Street counted the riches of heaven and
the chasms of the city streets deepened and beckoned before
her. The ship trumpeted and turned and thudded to a halt
in a commotion of small craft, amid the condescensions of
more lordly liners. Its flanks opened and the tide of curiosity
poured out. Nine hundred and eight passengers disappeared
in nineteen minutes. To the land of opportunity they seemed
to have brought nothing but their hands. Before Nalini
could accustom herself to the dynamic tempo of events in

the new order, she found herself alone on the pier with a Customs officer, brawny as a stevedore, balefully eyeing her seventeen pieces of luggage.

'What's all this for?' he asked. 'You going on an expedition up the Amazon?'

'Oh no,' said Nalini. 'I'm going to live on the Hudson for three years.'

He sighed theatrically. It was a habit she learned to like in Americans. They might over-act a trifle, but they made plain what they meant.

'Lady,' he explained to her, 'this is the Yewnighted States.'

'I know,' said Nalini. 'I know it's a wonderful country. But the trouble is, it's so far away from home.'

He tried again. 'What you got in there that can't be had at Macy's?'

'I've got clothes,' she said blandly.

'Just clothes ? You got nothing but clothes in seventeen king-sized cases?'

'Well, there are morning saris and evening saris and saris for summer and winter and coffee and tea and for taking trips upon buses and in case anyone whom I know gets married. In Madrasi silk and Benares and georgette and chiffon. And bronzes and brass and things out of which to eat things. And *atta* and *maida* and *dalda* and *cholis* and chillies and *chappals*. And a sweet little box containing *kunkumum* and *mye*. And two jars of American face cream – I suppose it was silly to have brought them.'

'I see,' he said sadly. 'I guess you got no gifts.'

'Oh no, I couldn't possibly afford them.'

44

He looked at her, still doubtful. 'You see, sir,' she said humbly, 'this is a wonderful country and I want it to be my home. But not so much that I can't remember my own home. I want some of where I came from to be alive where-ever I stay. So I've brought things to remind me. Yours is a wonderful country, officer, so it needs a lot of things to make one a little home-sick.'

He had to let her through after that. She smiled grate-fully at him, cascaded down an escalator and handed a pursuing gorilla ten dollars under a sign that said positively no tipping. He looked at her voraciously.

'What's happening to my luggage?' she managed to squeak.

'We're gonna look after everything, sister,' he leered.

A car crash-landed in front of her with a spine-chilling shriek of its brakes. It was brilliantly camouflaged, and to judge from its condition must have seen service at El Alamein. She scrambled into it. It shot off, riveting her to the rear squab. A notice on the partition advised her to sit back, relax and place her future in the experienced hands of Mr Saul Sokolsky, local nine billion eight hundred and forty-two. Next to the reassurance was a confidence-inspir-ing portrait of Mr Sokolsky. He looked as if he had just escaped from Sing Sing. He also drove maniacally as if the F.B.I. were after him.

'Riverside Drive, please,' said Nalini feebly.

Sokolsky made a desperate attempt to screw the steering-wheel off and, having failed narrowly, pushed the brake through the floorboard. Then he shoved the accelerator after it. The car rocketed into the sunshine out of a cleft of apartment houses. Nalini just avoided being flung against the front seat.

'Strike two,' a voice said, out of the middle dial.

Sokolsky swore softly and fingered the fat above his collar.

'I'm gonna hit the highway,' he announced. 'It's longer, but you get where you want to faster.'

Half an hour later and three blocks farther up, Saul Sokolsky was still hitting the highway along with two and a half million other time-saving motorists. The figures on the meter were beginning to read like the fare for a trans-atlantic crossing. Nalini started to fume; a bullock-cart at home would have been several times quicker. There was a burst of applause; she leaned out of the window, but saw no sign of the Mayor or the F.B.I. The noise was coming out of everybody's radio sets. Sokolsky shook his fist in the direction of the Bronx.

'Mays is slumpin',' he announced despondently.

Nalini was impressed. She knew that the Americans were a wide-awake people, but, even so, it was refreshing to find a cab-driver using his spare time on the West side highway to initiate a discussion on farm prices.

'Send some of it to Asia,' she suggested.

Sokolsky scratched his head. It was a hell of a long way for even Mays to hit a homer.

'You got me wrong,' he said. 'He's only been hitting two eight two.'

Sing Sing again, Nalini thought with a shudder. The slump had been only a brief slackening of sadism. She wondered what two eight two was like – a mild-mannered embezzler probably, who only wanted to send his children to Yale. It was sickening to think of him being pounded into pulp by a collection of dope fiends and frustrated all-in wrestlers.

'Maybe he'll see things differently,' she said.

'You bet he will,' cried Sokolsky. 'And when he sees 'em he'll smite 'em. When he gets hot he's gonna moider da bums.'

The glee with which he said it appalled Nalini even more than the blood-curdling content of the prophecy itself. She shrank back shivering in a corner, as Sokolsky with hair-raising dexterity steered the car through a momentary opening in the traffic. Curses exploded round him like misfiring cylinders as he headed furiously for the Seventy-ninth Street exit. The engine wailed resignedly as he hurtled up the hill, taking the starch neatly out of a jay-walker's shirt-front.

'High and inside,' the radio commented.

He skidded to a halt in front of her future home. She got out and looked apprehensively about her. It was a desolate haunt around which the wind whistled in spine-chilling and cinematic gusts. Scraps of newspapers and abandoned contraceptives waltzed grimly and obscenely round her ankles, howling their headlines on the latest rape case. Two louts were standing by the edge of a cliff, uncertain whether to admire the slaughter or to take part in it. She trembled at the thought of her fate, remembered her ancestors, and decided that if she must die she would at least die bargaining. She gave Sokolsky no more than a mere ten dollars.

'You got nothing smaller?' he asked.

She saw his face for the first time. It was more human

47

than his photograph. In fact his eyes had a touching loyalty about them which she learned to recognise later as the look of a man in love with a losing ball club.

'It doesn't matter,' she said, relieved. 'You're welcome to keep the change.'

The money was in his pocket long before the words were out of her mouth. 'I'll take your grips into the lobby,' he offered.

She had only a vanity-case and a copy of the *New Yorker*. He put them on a stool in front of the lift. Then he looked at her with sudden curiosity. His eyes went over her green sari and her hammered gold necklace and the circle of yellow brimming out of her hair, struggling not to be swept away by its dark weight. For the first time he was seeing Nalini herself and not the traffic, the fifth inning score, or the fare on the meter.

'Say,' he observed acutely, 'you must be a foreigner, ain't you?'

'Oh no,' said Nalini, her perkiness returning. 'I've lived here all my life.'

His jaw dropped. 'No kiddin',' he said, delightedly. 'The things they do at Bergdorf's.'

He pressed the call button. Bells rang, lights flashed, a door clanged open and an ancient denizen of the West side tumbled out.

'16 C, please,' said Nalini.

The apparatus whizzed upward, shuddered to a halt and pranced up and down in front of the landing while the operator fiddled with his levers.

'Mind the step,' he said in the end.

Nalini picked her stomach out of her feet and clambered out cautiously. The door of 16 C was open. There was a woman in the foyer in a nylon house-coat with Titian hair that was mouse-brown at the roots. She had an expansionist derrière which her corset frustrated.

'Abe,' she said, without turning. 'You haven't forgotten the pickles?'

'My name's not Abe, it's Nalini.'

She swivelled around. 'Nobody can pronounce that. My name's Marianne Schultz. My friends all call me Nan. Do your friends call you Nell?'

She smiled lavishly. She had three gold teeth in addition to other kinds of costume jewellery. A good deal of life seemed to have been pickled in her face, or what one could see of it beneath the make-up. She had grey-blue eyes with rings of hospitality beneath them, balanced by eyebrows like Venetian arches. Her mouth was generous also, assuming that it was half as large as the one she had painted with her lipstick. There was a pleasant aura of fair-mindedness about her; she was obviously a woman who insisted on giving no less than she received.

'I'm going to call you Nell, anyway,' she said. 'You're East Indian, aren't you, honey?'

'I'm South Indian,' Nalini corrected her.

She shrugged her shoulders and nearly dislodged her house-coat. 'I meant you aren't Red Indian. But wherever you came from, honey, you're an eyeful. Take it from me, you're going to wow the customers.'

By now Nalini was experienced enough to realise that such talk was not necessarily the prelude to her being spirited away into the white slave traffic. Under her land-lady's gold-plated exterior, she told herself, there was almost certainly a seven-carat gold heart. Reassured by this conviction, she smiled her most trusting smile and was rewarded by having Marianne's left arm wrap itself round her like a boa-constrictor.

'I'll show you your room now, honey,' she purred in her most persuasive and lava-like contralto.

It was a delicious room, Nalini thought. There was a glass shelf in one of the corners, with a plastic skirting in a bilious floral pattern, under which she could see the crumpled edge of a hat-box. The dresser was solid Eighth Avenue maple, hand-rubbed and initialled by previous lodgers with an ingenious, custom-made pattern of missing knobs. In front of the radiator was a beer-coloured carpet. The bed was painted canary yellow; it was covered by a vermilion spread that had apparently been used to clean a vacuum-cleaner. Nalini stroked it unbelievingly and a cloud of dust rose into the air like incense.

'Chenille,' the landlady said aloofly.

Nalini coughed and opened the window. The handle fell clattering to the floor. A gust of hamburgers blew in from the opposite apartment. On the floor above a woman with blonde hair in a heliotrope house-coat was showing a customer a canary-coloured bedspread.

'Yeah, I know it isn't the Ritz,' Marianne conceded. 'But for forty-four fifty what else can you get facing the river?'

'It's gorgeous,' said Nalini. 'I've never seen anything like it.'

Marianne looked suspicious. 'Don't think you can get it

for thirty-nine ninety-five. A Chinaman saw it yesterday. And a Mexican's coming tonight. For forty-eight fifty what else can you get with cross ventilation and a dramatic view of the New Jersey skyline?'

'But of course I want to take it,' Nalini said.

'Two-year lease and four and half years' security.'

'I'm afraid you'll have to discuss that with my father.'

Marianne Schultz thought it over. 'I guess you'll be O.K.,' she concluded. 'You've got an honest face. And there's no place you can go in that gipsy outfit. Seeing as you're a foreigner, I'll ask my lawyer friend Blitz Blatsky to figure out some way of evading the legal rental requirements of the City of New York.'

'Nan, honey,' Nalini crooned. 'I'll never live long enough to be able to thank you.'

'Nell, honey,' Marianne cooed back, 'for forty-six fifty you'll have to find your own soap.'

'But gas and electricity are included, aren't they?'

'For forty-seven eight five you get utilities, a free copy of yesterday's *Post* and a built-in retainer for the services of Blitz Blatsky.'

'It's a deal,' said Nalini.

'It's a fraud,' said Marianne Schultz. 'You drive a mean bargain with that please-look-after-me smile of yours. I don't know why I'm taken in by it. I guess it's because I've a secret passion to go bankrupt.'

She ambled off and paused charitably in the doorway.

'Have a nice time, honey,' she said. 'And if you want something, yell. I've a special friend who's going out of business. Name it and he can do without it. He can sell you anything including your front teeth – at prices you'd give your teeth for. They make Klein's basement look like the Empire State building.'

When she had gone, Nalini lay down entranced on the blissful luxury of her kapok-stuffed mattress, with a vagrant coil spring boring into her shoulder-blades. She inhaled the pastrami-laden air and the cinders blowing in from the smoke-stacks of New Jersey. The setting sun gilded the river and opened out her room, dissolving its walls and melting away its windows. She looked outside and pulled in what she saw to her heart. It was always brilliant in her memory after that, a picture that came back with the sound of klaxons, reminding her of the din of the traffic beneath, the fat man swilling beer in front of the TV, the beep of the great liners nosing up the rivers and the serene constellation of the bridge hanging in the night sky.

In the evening she descended into the depths, filled with a sense of patriotism for her new home. She entered a restaurant that was aggressively American. Fine-looking types from Italy, Hong Kong and Trinidad were propped obligingly against the architecture, preventing it from collapsing into the street. She seated herself precisely on a swivelling stool that was designed for someone with fourteen and a half inch hips. She disdained to reach for the menu; she had already read articles about American cuisine and knew what she should order to qualify as a citizen.

'I'll have Boston clam chowder,' she said, 'and roast, stuffed, young Vermont turkey. With golden-brown, melt-in- your-mouth Idaho potatoes. And king-sized, tree-ripened California peaches.'

'We got chop suey,' the girl said, 'and Swedish meat balls and Swiss steak. But we ain't got none of the fancy stuff you're wanting.'

'Then I'll have a hamburger,' Nalini insisted, doggedly.

'You want it with French fries?'

'I want it,' said Nalini, clenching her pretty teeth, 'with potatoes that taste of American earth, fried in the only way they should be, in butter fresh as a New England welcome. And then I'll have pie like your grandmother used to bake it when America was real and itself.'

'You mean, home fried,' the girl reproved her. 'Why don't you say so instead of letting your hair down? And the pie's ten cents extra with French ice-cream.'

With a sigh of resignation, Nalini settled down to her international repast. When it was over, she took again to the roads of discovery. A tree-ripened smile beckoned to her from the shop window opposite. She walked up and looked cautiously into the face. It belonged to a man with a Louisiana shrimp complexion.

'I want some Palestinian oranges,' Nalini said. She had learned her lesson well. To be truly American one had to be exotic.

'What's wrong with Florida?' the man demanded grimly.

'I'm sorry,' she apologised. 'I've been on the wrong side of the street. I'll take a half-dozen, sun-drenched, passion-kissed tangerines.'

He looked at her approvingly. 'You sure know what's good for you.' He tossed some photogenic fruit into a bag and played an amorous tune on his cash register. 'They're sixty-eight cents a dozen and worth double. Wrapped in cellophane to seal in the goodness. Want anything else, honey? The egg plant today is super-special.'

Her faith in America was restored. Here was a civilisation that grew eggs instead of hatching them. It seemed rather a pointless thing to do, but creative energy in its nature often had to be pointless. Although she was not enthralled by the thought of potential omelettes sprouting all over her bedroom, she realised that sacrifices had to be made for progress.

'I'll take two of them,' she said.

She was relieved as well as delighted when the egg plant turned out to be her familiar friend the *brinjal* without which no South Indian dinner was complete. And in another bin enigmatically labelled *Okra* she discovered lady's fingers as choice as any that her mother had fried in Mudalur. She could eat like an Indian now and still be American. There was no need to resort to Boston baked beans.

Her luggage arrived the same afternoon, miraculously intact. She scrubbed her room to receive it as if she were polishing a jewel and then filled every corner with flowers and bronzes and lustre that seemed to inhale the flashing lights outside. Like many people who come from nondescript houses she had learned to treasure her belongings, to see their essence intensely, to fling herself into them from the surrounding drabness. It needed little for her to make a place glow and soon the shabby eyrie was filled with the sense of the past and the feeling of her own life, looking across the sheen and smoke of the river or craning down into the gridiron of the streets. Everything in front of her bloomed with promise. The cliffs opposite were the outposts of a continent, and the Hudson was like the great rivers of India, broad and majestic and peopled with gods, even if only from Albany. She enjoyed descending into the city's winking gorges and letting her imagination dance amid the stuttering excitement of the great signs. When the morning dawned, smoke-filled yet antiseptic, she was down early, before the shadows had been peeled back from the river, revealing the sunlight with which she always knew the water had been mixed. She picked her way expertly among the dustbins, pausing for a moment to admire the great disintegrator with the infinite appetite as it clanged and churned and crushed away all misfortune, powdering the air with a faint cologne of garbage. In her hygienic haven of Formica she sat bolt upright on her Boltaflex stool, wedged in by attacking elbows, and ordered her toast with refined determination amid nationalistic shouts of English and Danish. 'Side of down,' the waitress screamed. Nalini smiled unconcernedly back; on a day like this she could eat even a second-hand bolster. She was a little disappointed when she received only what she had asked for. But she ate it frantically like everyone else and then scalded her throat ceremonially with coffee, having badgered three thimblefuls of 'cream' out of the waitress. She stepped out and joined the armoured column that was equipping itself with copies of the *Times* and *Tribune*. She bought both, positioned herself behind her shield of en-lightenment, was sucked into the vortex, biffed around a turnstile, and just avoided being flung on the rails in front of the sausage-shaped behemoth that drew up, jaws open, to receive its filling. She plunged into it and it plunged into the darkness. She looked around her to the extent that her position allowed. Grotesque shapes were everywhere huddled

55

into seats or crucified on doorways in varying attitudes of despair. But they were unified by a common humanity. They all read newspapers even if they had to suspend themselves from the ceiling to do it. She was touched by this devotion to knowledge. She wrapped herself like a mummy in her own texts. At 110th Street she emerged from her chrysalis, her eyes almost smarting from the sky's sudden blueness, and walked up the hill to the temple of learning, her mind vibrating with an expectancy that never left her no matter how often she repeated the journey. She had the natural seriousness for learning; knowledge to her still remained a way of becoming alive. There was a stubborn unity in her make-up so that a good book made her happy in the same way as a beautiful sari. But in her home the eagerness had grown into anxiety. Her mind had been diligently hammered into shape. The proper humility had been plastered over it and respect for authority was supposed to shine from its facets. The elders were always right because they were older and what was most ancient was certain to be most true. So she had learned to quote scripture for her purpose. Before she walked up the hill she had already studied many teachers, arming herself with every detail of their opinions so that she could speak firmly with the weight of recognised voices. For her guru she had reserved her most loving efforts at identification. She had admired him across two continents. His succession of books, heavy and lofty, in the coveted drabness of their university press bindings, were giant instalments in her progress to knowledge. She had read them all, far into the night, taking down the best of his wisdom in her note-books, the humane conclusions judicious rather than eloquent, the fastidious antitheses balanced upon the facts, the sarcasm used only when the wound was deserved. She was familiar with his face, with the acute features sharpened by intellectual unrest, with the gentle, shrewd eyes that always looked through and never resented error. When she came before him she was a little disappointed. Perhaps he was a little too much like the man who had not bothered to give her his seat in the subway. His clothes were chaotic rather than casual. He did not suggest a pattern of rebellion. The lack of tidiness and the impression of tiredness disconcerted her, but she told herself that the reality of the man was in his books and excited despite her reservations, in his presence, she put her work before him, devoutly in his image, in the exact words his learning had picked out, letting it live in the mould of his own brilliance. He listened with no hint of recognition. Then he turned on his reflection and destroyed it with an impartial efficiency that was even more like him than the image he had erased. But she couldn't understand that at first. She had to fight down her tears of humiliation. Both her idol and herself had been demolished. The dedicated mimicry of many months had been laid waste. Nothing was left but a wall of scepticism with not even an illusion to project upon it.

'They're your words,' she protested. 'They're the very words you used. I've read them again and again and I know them exactly. If you don't believe me I can quote you the page number.'

'You don't have to,' he said. 'I haven't forgotten what I put down. In fact, I'm not allowed to. But you mustn't act as if what I wrote is sacred.'

Her eyes brightened a little. 'You've changed your position then. It must have been quite recently. In the *Quarterly* last October there wasn't any hint of it.'

'Oh no,' he said categorically, 'my position hasn't changed.'

She felt he was amused and that didn't make her less angry.

'In that case what are you criticising me for? I've memorised all the facts. I've tried to put down all the arguments. I've even stated L's case and your reasons for not accepting it. If there's something I've left out, some way in which I haven't done your point of view justice –'

'There's nothing,' he assured her. 'You've put it all down exactly. I've never shaved before a more revealing mirror.'

'Then you're playing with me,' she said, 'or trying to show me my ignorance. You don't have to. I know how little I know and I've come here to change that. I'll study all your works, and the works of all recognised scholars in the subject. I'll familiarise myself completely with what they think.'

'It isn't a question of what they think,' he said. 'It's what you think that matters.'

'I don't see what that has to do with it.'

'I'm supposed to be your teacher, aren't I? It's your mind that I'm expected to train.'

'Then your business is to tell me what you know and what other authorities know. I promise to listen. I've come all this distance only to listen.'

'My dear girl,' he said gently, 'before you can really learn anything, you must first learn how to learn. Your mind isn't a sponge, mopping up information. It ought to be a kind of light, shining into the facts and revealing their pattern. Look after your intelligence and learn to use it responsibly. It's the little core of difference that makes you yourself. If you didn't own it, then everything else would own you.'

He looked at the words dropping into her mind. Then the happiness came to her eyes and he knew she had understood.

'I'm trying to teach you,' he said. 'I'm trying to talk to a person, not to a filing system or a calculating machine. Under the avalanche of facts – it feels like that sometimes, doesn't it? there's a creative force buried in you just as in anyone else. I want to reach it and to help it to grow.'

She was beginning to smile now, a smile both cautious and eager, her fingers on the door she had always been taught not to open.

'It's funny,' she said, 'suddenly being told that what you think makes any difference. It's a queer and bewitching and radiant sort of feeling. And you of all people had to give it to me.'

'What's so odd about that?' he asked. 'If I couldn't do that at least once every semester I'd give up teaching and become a garage mechanic.'

'Well, I've been taught by others,' she said. 'I've been squashed and squashed ever since I was four years old. And I've always been told that the squashing was for my own good. "Listen and don't argue," my teachers used to say. "Great minds have come to these conclusions. Who are you to presume to differ from them? Be humble and open yourself to their truth. When you grow older you'll find out what it all means." All this was from people who hadn't a tenth of your learning. They made me feel so small. So when I learned that I was to study under you I felt both happy and frightened. I read and memorised as I had never done before. I was preparing to be squashed once and for all. You did that in a way. But you've also helped me to stand up and none of my Indian sages ever did that.'

'Your teachers were deplorably un-Indian,' he said. 'I've read your philosophy on the way in from Mount Vernon. Not much of it, of course, and unfortunately in the wrong language. But isn't the essence of it that knowledge is within one and that you reach it by peeling off the various layers of illusion? Getting at the truth is a high-class form of strip-tease.'

'Of course not,' she said hotly. 'There's all the difference in the world between exhibition and discovery.'

He nodded in approval. 'A neat distinction, that. Too simple to serve long, but it makes a good beginning. I'm glad to find that I'm beginning to teach you.'

'Thank you very much indeed, sir,' she said.

He looked at her sharply. But she was not trying to mock him. Her eyes were bright, her expression quietly happy. She pressed her hands together in the *namaskar*, a gesture which touched him first by its artlessness and then made him feel like a religious institution. He consulted his watch and sent her on her way.

She skipped down the stairs into the street. 'You matter, you matter,' her heels said on the pavement. It was raining, the sodden leaves drifted across the street, the gutters gurgled with soot and yesterday's headline, yet never in her heart had she seen such a beautiful evening. Once again she was squashed in the churn of the subway, but her tormentors were only the ghosts of other teachers, so she smiled serenely at them, mummified in her magazines, as the L.R.T. thundered southwards for her alone. She moved up the stairs and into the festoons of light and stood at their centre, bathed in revelation, oblivious of the rôtisserie and its infra-red Adonis. She had found herself and the world moved round herself. The diadem of the city blazed unfalteringly for her. New York was for anyone who put ten cents in its turnstile.

She came to know the city in many moods. In winter she plodded through the streets, incognito, between a pair of ear-muffs half as large as her face while the snowflakes whirled before her like confetti falling in front of a movie star. She lifted her sari up to her calves like a flamenco dancer, trying to keep the border out of the slush. Upstairs she drank hot, tinned soup, embraced the central heating and shivered comfortably after hearing the weather forecast. Spring came and she had never seen anything like it. The leaves grew on the trees almost as fast as a housing development. She admired the blossoms in their promise, vivid and delicate, with a transience of colour so unlike the imprisoned, constant richness of her own forests. She walked in the sunshine through their fallen loveliness to her favourite viewpoint, the Cloisters, looking down at the dark-green origins of Manhattan, the warehouses and grimy sidings of the Bronx and at the Hudson, straightforward and unruffled, receding into the continent like a ninety-eight lane highway. In the summer too, she learned to love the city, where the prices recklessly fell as the temperature mounted, and the air-conditioners purred their blandishments in the huge, empty department stores, and the cinemas moaned of passion in their cool depths. She listened to the statistics pouring out of the Battery and watched the endless line of escaping automobiles crawling towards their freedom endlessly and joyously, towards the clover leaves and bow knots of the parkways. She herself joined in this universal ritualised insanity, inched furiously through five miles in four hours and desperately drove two hundred in three and a half. She dined bucolically on frozen meat and canned beer. She saw four cows, but they were all on billboards. She came back inspiringly full of exhaust gases, with tail-lamps flashing excitingly in front of her eyes and with a deep sense of achievement which was beyond explanation but which she knew made her a party to the American way of life. She was drawn to the many-sidedness of New York, to the turbulent harmony of its tongues and races, to the mammoth stores that refused to be undersold and the small shops perpetually pretending to go out of business, to the manner in which the sombre monument of the city's stone age jostled uninhibitedly against the shining triumphs of its age of aluminium. She liked the people with their welcoming, decent vulgarity, their worship of children and cheesecake, their demented escapes into week-end mirages, their homely dedication to the twenty-one inch dream. She was struck by their hospitality, by the manner in which people she had only just met opened their homes to her and made her one of their own. Intense shipboard friendships she thought them at first – the casual tents offered by a nation of nomads – but she found permanence in them and came to appreciate the different worlds behind the uniform picture windows.

Yet when she collected her impressions and tried to arrange

them round a centre of significance it was not the size and
spectacle of the city that mattered, the turbulence that seethed
and foamed in its clefts, the perpetual movement, the building and rebuilding, the exuberance of prosperity, so often
aimless and gaudy, but at its best creating the power to be
oneself; it wasn't the two million automobiles, the great
bridge of which the revenue was more than her country's
budget, the enormous and enthralling Sunday newspapers
which took all human curiosity for their province; it wasn't
even the people, raucous and generous, voluble and self-
critical, undressing their policies in scandalised, endless
debates, unused to great responsibilities, anxious to be liked,
a people obliged to commute into history, who wanted to be
happy, not to govern. When she thought of America these
were the memories that came back first, but when she thought
more intensely, they receded, and there was only a room like
any other study, an ordinary face behind drugstore spectacles,
a matter-of-fact voice reciting obvious truths which came
alive, which suddenly made her real, which were the glow
and essence of the image she took away, the will to be herself, the most self-evident and the most sky-scraping dignity.

'You matter, you matter', the wheels in the subway had
said, and now with the oceans recrossed and the train thrusting into her country's blazing distance, the wheels of her
carriage had said it again, endlessly, reassuringly, beating
the truth into the sterile plains. She was coming back now,
not just to a different land but to a different self. The half-
world of separation had been traversed. The fond farewells
had been washed away by the distance, the skyline and the
streets and the floodlit prosperity had receded behind the

plate glass of her memories and what lived was the heat, and the cries of the vendors of sweetmeats, the beggar's maimed arm, the emaciated bullock dredging the well, the approaching hills where she would have to defend her reality against the exactions of the family ideal.

But the test was yet to come and meanwhile the present was not uncomfortable. She was alone in a compartment half as large as her New York bedroom. She lay back, relaxing on her elbows, knowing that her feet would never again be frostbitten, letting the contentment of the past flow over her. The sights and the smells and the sounds she had known came back, each with its own caress of familiarity. She let them flirt with her senses. Remembrance was more exciting than discovery if one had been far enough away to half-forget.

The train whistled and snorted and made reluctant preparations to leave. The guard walked down the platform, waving his flag. There was the usual succession of banging doors, and relatives who had come to say farewell tumbled out of compartments with mild squeaks of alarm. A man rounded the corner behind the second-class waiting-room, running with a loping, leisurely stride as if slightly contemptuous of the abilities of the engine. He headed for Nalini's carriage and opened the door. The porter behind him pointed vainly to the sign and shouted out, but the young man did not hear him. He trotted by the train as it began to move slowly forward, wailing and gesticulating in a torment of apprehension, as if a seduction were about to take place. The young man flung open the window and pulled his suitcase and bedding roll out of the porter's arms.

He threw a two-anna piece on to the platform. The porter stopped crying and began to curse. He launched into a virulent description of the many sins committed by the young man's ancestors. He called upon the God Siva to abandon all his other preoccupations and to focus his third eye urgently on this particular miscreant's head. The train gathered speed, left the porter behind, and burst with relief out of the clouds of his invective.

'You don't mind my being here, do you?' the young man asked.

'You must be a college student,' Nalini said. It was always the first thing she associated with bad manners.

'First class, right through,' the young man proudly proclaimed. 'Highest marks for the last ten years in my district.'

'And you still don't even know how to read.'

'Was there something I ought to have read?'

'This is a ladies' compartment,' Nalini said a little impatiently.

'Ladies! Oh dear! Well, it's too late to get out now. And anyway it doesn't matter, does it? These dainty distinctions are becoming out-of-date. You've got the vote now and you'll have to pig it with us.'

'Pig it' wasn't inappropriate at all, Nalini thought. He had a soup-stained moustache and a thirty-six-hour growth of stubble. His hair was plastered and reeked of coconut oil. There was a faint smear above his heart where his fountain-pen had leaked into his shirt. But with less hair and more soap one could have been aware of the character in the intense eyes and of the well-proportioned face which might even have been suave if the man had been better fed. His mouth too would have been sensitive, had it not been overawed by the fungus.

'Which university are you from?' he asked.

He wanted to seem perspicacious and it was a safe assumption that she was a student, since she was young and evidently unmarried.

'Columbia, New York,' she answered a little haughtily. She had no real inclination to seem uppish about it, but his behaviour had stung her into an appearance of pride. She looked out of the window to heighten the effect.

'Hmmm!' the young man said dubiously. 'Been away from India long?'

'You can't do your degree in less than three years.'

'It's far too long,' the student told her gloomily. 'We're independent now. We've different attitudes and different standards. We're Indians, not mimics of the white man. We've changed and you've changed, but in the wrong direction. You won't fit in. You've joined the lost generation, out of place everywhere and acceptable nowhere. You'll always be an exile and an alien, a self-created foreigner, a refugee from yourself. You can't belong. You'll live in two worlds and fall between two stools.'

He paraded the synonyms as evidence of his wide reading, the accumulation adding to the crushing weight of his argument.

'Oh fiddlesticks!' said Nalini warmly. 'All this belonging is balderdash. This is my country and I like the way it looks. And if I don't like anything, I'll make it what I like.'

'That isn't Indian either,' said the young man. 'Too

rebellious an attitude. You'll never get married if you go on thinking like that.'

'What can a weed like you possibly know about marriage?'

'I should know a great deal,' he said. 'My name is Kalyanasundaram.'

He treated himself to a delighted burst of laughter.

'Yes, I know. The name means "beautiful marriage". But it's only a name, so what does that prove?'

'You haven't asked me what I do,' he said.

She didn't ask, so he proceeded to tell her.

'I'm a specialist in arranged marriages.'

'Show me an Indian who isn't.'

'You misunderstand me,' he explained. 'I don't arrange them. I explore them. I dissect them. My occupation is to answer those newspaper ads. Particularly the ones that are really desperate. You know, the ones that say: "Caste no bar, university degree not essential." That's a sure sign of approaching panic. Then I write in and of course my caste is everything that it should be and my academic qualifications are above reproach. It's really a wonderful way to earn a living. Free board and lodging and the red carpet treatment. And most of the time my rail fares are paid in advance.'

'It's as simple as that?' she asked, a little disgusted. 'They don't even ask for a photograph?'

'More often than not they're so eager that they don't. That's the point of picking the desperate ones. But if they insist on something then I send them this.'

He fished a photograph out of his wallet and showed it to her. It looked remarkably like a picture of Ramon Novarro. The resemblance to the young man was less striking, but perhaps real enough to save him from being sued for having sent it.

'You write to these poor people,' Nalini said, trying to fight back her anger. 'You take their money. You live like a lord in their homes. And all the time you haven't the slightest intention of doing the thing in which you express an interest. The last thing you're prepared to do is marry.'

'Oh, I wouldn't say that,' Kalyanasundaram protested. 'I'm quite prepared to marry – in principle, that is. And I'm pretty broad-minded about it. I don't care how ugly or fat the bride is, if the dowry is big enough and the car is American and the girl has been trained to shut up and say yes to her husband. In a way, the uglier she is the better. It gives me a reason to go out and forget. Of course, I'm prepared. It's just that I'm not yet ready to jump into the furnace.'

'You're never going to be ready,' Nalini burst out. 'You'll never be, because you're a fraud and a parasite.'

'How dare you!' said the young man. His indignation was genuine and surprising. 'Do you think I'm doing this just to amuse myself?'

'You're certainly not amusing anyone else.'

'My motives are not frivolous. If distress is inflicted I'm sorry. I try to make the pain as little as possible. It is necessary in the pursuit of knowledge.'

'Knowledge!' echoed Nalini. She was sceptical but not uninterested. Her hand, which had been moving up to the communication cord, came down.

'Yes, knowledge!' the young man passionately declared. 'Knowledge to fight the arranged marriage, to expose it in all its revolting nakedness, its threats, its bribes and its pitiful

68

desperations. Knowledge with which to destroy this malig-
nant canker which is eating out the heart of Hindu society.'

'Hear, hear!' applauded Nalini. 'I'm all on the side
of that speech. Even though it probably isn't you who
made it.'

'Of course it's I. Just because I make my living out of the
truth, don't think I'm not a crusader and an idealist.'

'But you're prepared to marry someone fat and ugly.'

'If one eats with the devil one must pay his price. I too
am a child of the evil I condemn. But that does not mean
that one should not condemn it.'

'And how,' asked Nalini, 'is this process of condemning to
take place? This salacious unveiling of the truth in its shocking nakedness?'

'You mock me,' the young man warned her, 'because you
think it can't happen to you, you with your Western freedom.
But you too can have nose-rings fixed in your delicate nostrils
and be led by them, trussed up, to your abandonment.'

'If that ever happened, I'd soon do something about it. I
wouldn't sit there waiting for you to save me.'

'I wouldn't presume to do so. My forum is larger than the
individual. A mass disease demands a public remedy.'

'Get into Parliament and pass a law, then.'

'A law doesn't live in men's minds. But a book can and
mine will; not simply in their thoughts, but in their passions.'
He spoke the words with a caressing exultation, titillated by
the havoc that the power of his pen could wreak. 'To destroy
one must expose. One must lay bare an image to contempt
and ridicule. One must trample an idol in the market-place
so that never again will it rise up in men's visions.'

'And your book will achieve all that?' she wondered doubtfully.

'There is no acid more corrosive than the truth. I have assembled the facts. I have indexed the sordid histories. I begin with three hundred sample advertisements. Then I dissect the realities behind them. The snobberies of sects and sub-sects. The fabrication of horoscopes. The surrender of human fate to stellar caprice. The astrologers and the pundits. The financial reconnaissance. The discreet inquiries about distinguished relatives. The redemption of imbecility by wealth. The sin of poverty and the bribe of good looks. And the dowry. Always the dowry. The meanness, the humiliation, the degraded contract that seals the bargaining process. I've fifty-seven pages on the dowry alone.'

'It sounds devastating,' said Nalini, mildly malicious. 'You must have had dozens of offers for the book.'

'Oh, it isn't yet written,' the young man explained. 'It exists only in my mind. I have to put it into shape, to discipline my anger into a creative pattern. But when I do write it, it will shake the Vindhyas.'

'Well, they have to end,' Nalini said, more seriously. 'Arranged marriages, I mean. But I think people will come to recognise that by themselves. You don't have to lash them into seeing it.'

He shook his head. 'Society needs a scourge.' One could see his eyes glinting as pictures of chastisement danced enticingly before them. 'My book will provide the basis of disgust which is necessary for complete rejection. Everyone will buy it. The unmarried will see in it the banana skin on which they have not slipped. The married will learn from it not to inflict their sins upon their children. It will be compulsory reading in all examinations. Considering how large is the student population of India, my royalties will undoubtedly be colossal and will enable me to blaze still wider paths of destruction. Perhaps I can even make my own choice in marriage. Somebody sensible, rather like you, for instance.'

'I'm honoured indeed,' said Nalini, 'but I'm probably much too Westernised for your taste.'

'Oh, I can always teach you manners,' he assured her. 'The time isn't ripe though. The book has to be written. This is the age of anger, not of self-indulgence.'

'And you're undertaking this journey to make you even angrier.'

'This journey is unique,' the young man said. 'The father isn't like anyone I've studied. He won't even consider rail fares in advance. He refuses to send me her photograph or her horoscope. All that he will say is that the young lady can be seen and he promises that she is exactly as per advert.'

'And what does the advertisement say?'

Kalyanasundaram started to shake with laughter.

'It says she's an unprecedented paragon.'

It was Nalini's turn to smile.

'Oh well,' she concluded charitably. 'Every father believes that of his daughter.'

'Not if he seriously wants to get her married. And just look at where the old man chooses to live.'

'He doesn't live in Villipuram, does he?' She had stayed there once in a season of drought and her remembrance of it was peopled with grim memories.

'Villipuram,' the young man said scornfully. 'At least you

can find it in any atlas. To find out where *this* place is you need one of those special five miles to the inch jobs. At first I thought he must be a planter, no one else would live in so outlandish a hole. But I've been through the records of the Planters' Association and he doesn't grow tea or coffee or anything like that. So he isn't up there in order to make money. It must be because he hasn't any in the first place.'

'He's penniless and proud,' Nalini mused. 'And his daughter's beautiful too. It sounds like something out of a story book.'

'But he isn't desperate at all, that's what intrigues me. He acts as if his daughter is Draupadi and he's calling us there in order to hold a tournament.'

The train had been climbing steadily as they spoke, with the hills on each side crowding gradually closer, the flanks steepening as they neared the head of the valley. The engine hooted warningly as they entered the tunnel. No lights came on and they sat cautiously in the darkness, trying to clarify various ominous outlines. The engine whistled repeatedly as if scandalised by events. When the lights eventually functioned they were needed, even though the train was now on the other side. It was menacingly dark and the skies looked greenish, as if soaking up the colour of the forests that flowed on avidly down the slopes of the hills, seeming to blot them out by their sheer pressure. The air was thick and full of an intense life, heavy in a way that pushed one inwards. The first swollen drops fell, not even splashing the earth, but breaking open of their own gross weight. Then the downpour came, persistent, grey and solid. Even the wind, leaking rather than blowing through the forests, was barely able to stir the rain-drenched leaves. It was a business-like, professional operation, a methodical, monotonous saturating of the earth from which all distractions were sedulously excluded.

The train stopped opposite the stone and mud platform, too sodden for even its customary hoot. Above the platform was a narrow, galvanised-iron roof. The rain drummed on it in a deafening tattoo before cascading off it in a sheet of water through which the unfortunate passengers had to duck. It seemed incredible that anyone should find life worth living in the deluge but various people emerged with alacrity from nowhere and proceeded eagerly to do business with those in the ark.

Kalyanasundaram looked out of the window. He could see nothing through it but that did not make what he didn't see less distasteful.

'Try to think of something more depressing,' he suggested.

'Oh, I wouldn't say that,' Nalini disagreed. 'There are jewels of places hidden in those hills.'

The young man shrugged his shoulders.

'Well, I've asked for it, I suppose. Worse things can happen in the pursuit of knowledge. Depressing or not, this is where I have to get out.'

A disturbing suspicion took hold of Nalini.

'This is where I get off, too,' she informed him guardedly.

He wasn't aware of anything amiss.

'Use my umbrella,' he suggested. 'Yours is brand-new and we don't want the rain to ruin it.'

They scuttled out through the waterfall and under the corrugated roof. She was disappointed at finding no trace of her family, but remembered that her father was given to unpredictable tests of morale which in his didactic moments he compared irrelevantly to the ordeal of Sita. Perhaps, she told herself, he was trying to evaluate the self-reliance she should have acquired in America.

A porter, dressed only in a loin-cloth, shambled up to them, touching a non-existent hat. He began to extract from the carriage Kalyanasundaram's two pieces and Nalini's nineteen. The luggage was piled high till it dwarfed the two passengers. The porter did his work first incredulously, and then with an elation that mounted with the luggage. Never before had he achieved so much in one day. People flocked from all sides to admire his performance and to offer help which was indignantly refused. He completed his task and salaamed expectantly to Nalini. She gave him four rupees. He looked at the miracle, decided it was real, and broke out in jubilant praise of her heavenly radiance and of her pedigree back to the eighth ancestor. The others in the gathering salaamed even more copiously and began to inform Nalini at length of their present undeserved poverty, their past achievements and their ardent desire to perish in her service.

The owner of the best bullock-cart rubbed his hands. There were three others at the station, but his was the only one with a roof. He joined nominally in the chorus of deference but he was more concerned to calculate what the traffic would bear.

Kalyanasundaram looked resignedly at the four carts.

'You can take the covered one if you care to,' he told Nalini. 'I'll hang around here until the rain decides to stop.'

'I think we're both going the same way,' she said.

'It's quite impossible. I'm heading for an infernal dump called Mudalur. It's probably like its name too; mud everywhere with the rain mixing it up and a few thatched houses lurching drunkenly out of it.'

'It's where I live,' she said a little acidly.

His jaw dropped. 'You're Sambasivan's daughter? The girl in the ad? There must be some mistake. Why, you're not even half-way to being ugly.'

'Thank you. I try to live up to my notices.'

'Nobody,' he said, tactlessly, 'could ever live up to *that* one.'

'You're outrageously rude.'

'You're impossibly conceited.'

'It's my misfortune to have to ride with you in this cart.'

'I shall not deprive you of a pleasure you do not merit.'

They flounced in, looking away ostentatiously from each other. She set her chin a little. After three minutes of silence she was able to sense him glancing at her profile.

'You know,' he observed, 'when you're angry like that you're half-way to being beautiful.'

'In that case I hope always to madden you with my loveliness.'

'If you want to get married you might learn not to walk over an apology.'

'And you might learn to deliver one with grace.'

She felt mean after saying that and turned back to him.

'I'm sorry,' she said. 'I didn't really intend to be rude.'

'I can't understand it,' he persisted. 'The advertisement, I mean. When a girl is like you there's no need to advertise.

The less said the better, if you know what I mean.'

'I hope I never do,' she retorted icily.

He began to laugh. 'It's wonderfully ironic. Three years of a fancy education and now you're heading straight back into an arranged marriage. You'll be given away to some corpulent money-lender you've never even seen.'

'Nobody's going to push me around,' she flared back.

Her eyes flashed and he liked that. Then they softened suddenly and he liked that even more. The smile stole over her face, turning up the corners of her mouth gently.

Of course, arranged marriages were obsolescent, reactionary and inhuman. But they had their advantages too. It was nice to be called an unprecedented paragon. And to have hopeful young men churning their way up through the monsoon mud to find her. And to be Draupadi, presiding over a tournament.

II

Nothing invented could have kept out the rain. The soggy, saggy canopy above them yielded gradually to the assault and the water dripped through the weak points in the thatching, aiming maliciously at the nape of Nalini's neck. The steady trickle depressed her and made her think of Garbo, whom she did not greatly resemble. Then she remembered her habitual trudge through the snow, across the two blocks from the river to the restaurant, with the wind, knife-edged, whistling in from New Jersey's cold infinities. It was certainly better to be wet than frozen. The monsoon was a creative, fertilising force and she thought of it now, fingering its way down her back, almost charitably, as a salutation of the elements. She sat bolt upright since in America she had often listened to admiring compliments on the carriage of Indian ladies and on the peasant equilibrium which enabled them to carry large brass vessels for enormous distances on unfaltering heads. She had often watched her washerwoman perform this feat but until she left India it never struck her as a skill to be imitated. That was one of the advantages of exile; it gave one an intelligent sense of perspective so that a skinny individual clouting a drum on the wayside became suddenly an impassioned worshipper of a dark god.

She sat bolt upright as befitted her marvellous, instinctive sense of deportment and looked at her feet which, to tell the truth, were a little too large to be entirely admirable. Since she was the apple of her parents' eyes, fed upon coconut milk and pearls of wisdom, she was, it must be confessed, a trifle more robust than others just as well-born but not so fondly bred. But the lines of her body were fluent and one thought of her naturally as dainty and petite, not because the objective facts justified it but because there was something in her bearing that said so. It was a secret more native than the ability to carry large brass vessels and, fortunately, too soothing to be analysed. She looked at herself, candid and gentle, and supply sweet even in the rain's bedragglement, and felt that the stage had suffered a sad loss when she decided not to become a dancer. Then she reproached herself for being much too vain. Not feeling any drastic twinge of conscience, she started to admire her sari, largely because she was no longer angry with Kalyan and didn't want him to be too soon aware of that fact, It was a highly becoming sari like the one hundred and seventy-six others she possessed. Her father had taught her to throw nothing away, and when she appeared in some particularly radiant outfit it was good to describe it carelessly and truthfully as something forgotten and out-of-date which had lain negligently on a shelf for fourteen years.

Kalyanasundaram watched her watching herself and knew that her inward eyes were watching him. He was conscious of his scruffiness and of the rain smudging it further. Since he did not know what the bullock-cart was doing to her spine he saw her only as floating in a flourish of orange and violet which his eyes, he told himself angrily, were romantically hazing. It was impossible that she should have been corrupted by foreigners, this girl who survived a drenching so well and in whose hair the raindrops consorted with false diamonds. He tried to consider her dispassionately as a research project and arranged his mind in a series of pigeon-holes through which, to his mortification, her image floated intact. He glared out of the cart at the leaves flapping past his eyelashes, in a sodden, monotonous disgust.

'Kalyan,' he heard her saying, 'I don't want to disturb you, but there's a frog near your left elbow.'

He squirmed violently and ejected the creature. Then he realised that he had been startled not so much by its intrusion as by her familiarity in calling him Kalyan. This was truly the corruption of foreignness and, not knowing her first name, he could not repay her in kind.

'Thank you,' he said, refrigerating his voice. 'And whom

have I the honour of addressing?'

Her eyes glowed mischievously. She opened her handbag and gave him her card. This was getting worse and worse, he thought. He didn't have a card which he could hand back.

'I shouldn't speak to you,' he suggested aloofly. 'Not until your parents have introduced us. I shouldn't take advantage of our being in this cart.'

'You can always say what's on your mind, Kalyan. It's raining hard enough to wash away bad manners.'

'Now look, Nalini,' he began and flushed. The name felt far too much like honey on his tongue.

'I'm looking,' she said and disarmingly did so.

'I haven't decided whether I'm interested in you personally, or for the pursuit of knowledge.'

It was her turn to flush. 'You *can* be uncommonly rude.'

'If I've absolutely no chance with you then I'll get out of this cart.'

'I can't possibly tell,' she said. 'Not until I've got to know all the others.'

'You're enjoying this thoroughly, aren't you?'

'Must everyone in your wretched book be unhappy?'

'Arranged marriages,' he snorted. 'The people in them are dead. They're yoked together like bullocks at a funeral.'

'You can be absolutely certain that I wouldn't be found dead with you.'

'Ha! Ha!' he tittered ostentatiously. 'I know exactly what to call it. American-returned girl gives in to family juggernaut! It'll add at least ten thousand to my sales.'

He had begun to goad her, so to soothe herself she thought

of Draupadi and of a splendid young man bending a Gandiva bow. But the thought did not reassure her. She was realistic about her face and didn't expect it to launch a thousand ships; but it would have been flattering to daydream in the Western tradition, to have a valorous knight-errant flaunt her emblem and challenge all to combat on her behalf. Far more flattering certainly than being pawned like poor Draupadi at a dice game, merely to satisfy a warrior's code of conduct.

They rounded a bend and found that the road had subsided, the loose gravel cascading into the ravine below. There remained a crevice about three feet deep in which Sambasivan's cart was comically lodged. His inside wheel had careered into the ravine and the driver, who was reluctant to follow in pursuit of it, had maintained that the place was sacrosanct, being inhabited by a python, descended directly from the holy snake *Takshaka* himself. Sambasivan, who believed that every python had its price, was trying to determine the price of this one and to allow for the inflation caused by his daughter's arrival. Lakshmi stood on the cart platform, bewailing her lot triumphantly and ignoring the waterlogged plantain leaf which the wind periodically slapped into her face.

It was a fortunate accident, since the sunken cart now formed a natural bridge over which Nalini's own cart could negotiate the crevice in safety. They piled into the vehicle while the bullocks swished their tails in protest and the driver demanded an increase in his fare. Nalini explained Kalyanasundaram's presence, without mentioning his odd interests in research. Lakshmi stared at the stranger as if she were looking at a jackfruit and trying to decide whether

it was ripe for plucking. It was the baleful condescension of
the prospective mother-in-law that had seen all the deceits
and fallen through every trapdoor.

They were not the most resplendent of parents and they
didn't wear the monsoon as well as their daughter. But
watching them sit there bedraggled, with the rain and the
tears streaming down Lakshmi's face, watching her father's
smile in which benevolence had changed into inanity in trying to pose before an imaginary camera, Nalini had a feeling
of rightness that came close to contentment. She was surprised at the feeling and uncertain of its reality. Her life
had never been very close to her parents. She had not come
into the world easily and her mother, bearing the long
struggle with fortitude, had hoped to be rewarded with more
than a daughter. They had doted on her sporadically, out
of a sense of guilt. Then realising that she could not be a
son, they had tried to make her one in everything but sex.
She would carry forward the family name, surround it with
respect and give it lustre. In her mother's eyes she would
atone for all her father's failings.

Gopal was born five years later. The doctors gave Lakshmi
no chance, but she survived by an act of will which must
have communicated itself to the frail infant. Her body
accomplished its task, redeemed its deficiencies. Then she
lived more easily since no more could be asked. Gopal grew
up, the sap fighting its way weakly through the stranglehold
of illness after illness. His face was frozen. He moped by
the window, ate his meals in a trance. They looked after
him with an anger against circumstance that gradually
changed into an aloofness towards him. He was beautiful

in the way of sickly children. His eyes, having looked through many mists of pain, had an unnatural, penetrating brightness. But he learnt slowly, resisting every effort to teach him. Each thought had to be hammered into his mind until it became the scar of a new illness.

They turned back to Nalini from the blind alley of his birth and their fondness became demanding, inflexible, avid. There was a pattern to which she had to conform, the pride of her parents in her had to be justified and heavy responsibilities laid early on her slim shoulders. She was better than others and so she had more to accomplish. It was not sufficient to be head of the class. She had to lead everyone by an unprecedented margin. She would wake in the morning before the *kolum* was drawn in front of the house and pore unceasingly over the Sanskrit texts, trying to make the intoxication of the language a substitute for the early morning freshness that filtered only fitfully into her small room. In the evening through the barred windows, as the light fell, she could hear the shouts of the children playing. Inside the music teacher importunate, slapping his thigh, her voice going up and down and across the unending arrangements, till the subtleties of the music became a nightmare and a treadmill, another note wrenched from the despairing harmonium. Her head would throb mercilessly under the fifteen-watt lamp and her parents, with distant solicitude, would tell her to preserve her eyesight and improve her calculus, to eat more and to mope less, to be all the paradoxes which their tyrannies fondly evaded.

She was surprised when they sent her to America. Her father was determined to perfect the image, but her mother still thought that demons lived in Laṅka and that they became steadily worse as one went westwards. She had left to a chorus of cautions that might have suggested that home was an imprisonment. In a sense it was, in a sense she had been liberated by her three years in America, but though she realised what had happened even while it was happening, she was too well-balanced to be overthrown by her freedom. Her independence became more shapely and vigorous; but it did not challenge the past or overturn idols. She wrote to her parents regularly and fondly and when she took up her pen she was not often aware of the distance as an emptiness. Yet they belonged to a different life. And she was coming back to it a different person. She had to be ready for the shock of strangeness and not give herself up because the young always gave way; or rebel so violently that she trod on others' dreams. She had been trained well and she would have to walk the tightrope.

It was not until the meeting was over that she realised how she had braced herself to meet it. She had even worn the same sari as when she went away but with a difference that suggested the difference. Her father perused her vaguely, recognising that something was amiss, but attributed it to the ways of women and the effects of a foreign diet. Her mother looked at her more sharply, noticed the varnish on her fingernails and sniffed both dubiously and wistfully at the Chanel. They exchanged glances; although she had not shared all her mother's feelings they had often spoken to each other in this way and Nalini found it reassuring to slip back so easily into this second language.

Lakshmi's remembrances fingered her daughter's grace,

caught so rightly now in that precious balance of youth, not
taut, not blossoming, but gently, yieldingly green. She might
have been that herself once if she had grown up a little less
stumpy, a little less harried, if she hadn't come out of a mould
of drudges, grinding flour in the kitchen mortar, flogging
everyone else's clothes into cleanliness, on the glistening
stones beside the courtyard well. When she thought of Nalini
as her unachieved self, the passion of a lost dream reached
through her and she couldn't bear to think of her daughter
being given away. It was relinquishing even the reminder,
the painting she wanted to hang on the wall of her feelings.
She told herself, her lips trembling, that age stripped a
mother of everything, that whatever was given had to be
given away also. Nalini was grown up now, all that remained
of her past self was the sari. She was there to be looked at,
to be sought out, not to be set aside on the shelf of a promise.
She would enter a room hereafter, making it different, not
glide into it in a surprise of modesty. Tomorrow, she would
have to enter a house and to keep it hers as well as keep it
clean.

The cart groaned to a halt in front of Hillview and the
occupants tumbled out, steadying their cramped limbs. A
servant rushed forward carrying an umbrella which refused
to open and then blew inside out. They waded their way in
through the puddles. The house was full of the fragrance of
sandalwood, flowers and incense, which at this inauspicious
moment had only the effect of making everyone sneeze. The
cavalcade marched onwards, sprinkling with mud and water
the *kolums* that had been drawn at the entrance to each
circle. In the innermost regions they renewed themselves.

Dinner was served a little later. The men were the first to eat, in accordance with custom. Nalini had laid the table – or more correctly the floor – but she did not go to the extent of waiting on her guests. Custom required that also, but Lakshmi would have none of it. Having no high opinion of any of the suitors she felt that they should be locked up, fed through barred windows and rationed strictly in their access to the prospective bride.

The ladies ate later in an inferior circle. Lakshmi watched critically as Nalini sat down on her plank in the proper posture, the left leg in a horizontal, the right in a vertical hairpin. She accomplished the feat without visible anguish.

'Thank heavens,' said Lakshmi gratified. 'You haven't forgotten how to do that in America.'

'Oh, it isn't difficult, really. Not half as difficult as getting into a sports car.'

Her mother sniffed. 'Sports car, eh! It's part of your education to ride around in sports cars?'

Sin to her was synonymous with red leather.

'Not often,' said Nalini cautiously. 'Only to go from one place to another.'

Lakshmi seemed not to detect the evasion. She offered Nalini a portion of shredded wheat.

'We bought it specially for you.'

'I don't want it,' said Nalini. 'There are other things here which I'd much rather have.'

Lakshmi's face was beaming with satisfaction.

'We understand perfectly; it's the right spirit in you. But you mustn't try too hard. Little by little you can get used to things. We don't expect you to forget all your foreign habits

85

in one day.'

'I never ate cereals,' said Nalini smilingly.

'But, my poor girl, what on earth did you have for breakfast?'

'Oh, mostly fruit juice and toast.'

'Fruit juice and toast! Nalini, don't be ridiculous. It's the sort of meal that Gandhiji ate as a penance.'

'Well, millionaires' wives live on it in America.'

Lakshmi's eyes widened. Her hands started to move in semicircles of protest. She was about to give vent to the customary wail about her daughter's thinness when she looked at Nalini in the double hairpin shape and decided that her figure was nearly everything that it should be.

'Never mind, my jewel. We'll feed you properly here. You can have all the sweets and *Sambhar* that you want.'

She hoped that her daughter wouldn't take the assurance too literally. It would be so early to spoil a silhouette that American fads had made the embodiment of Indian woman-hood.

Nalini looked at the food in neat piles on her plantain leaf, the *Avial*, the *Sambhar*, the curling snake coils laced with shredded coconut, the rich tan of the dhal nestling beside the incredibly white, soft rice, and the backs of the *brinjals* glistening with melted butter. She mixed them together expertly and ardently with the true fervour of the returning exile. Her hand scooped up a portion of the nectar. Then her wrist flicked backwards and upwards gracefully, her tongue meeting her palm unhesitatingly at the precise moment when the food would otherwise have cascaded down her forearm. There was the delicate sucking sound that accompanied the operation when perfectly performed. The hand went down in a continuation of the same fluent, wristy motion and came up again, smooth and certain as a conveyor belt.

Lakshmi watched her daughter admiringly, delighted that her right hand had lost none of its ancient skill.

'I'm satisfied,' she said. 'I'm satisfied that you've forgotten very little. The only question is to find out what you've learned.'

III

It was not clear whether the suitors should be presented in alphabetical order, the order of their arrival, or in their presumed order of desirability. Sambasivan suggested that age should have precedence, or alternatively that priority be given to him who could shoot an arrow farthest or plant the largest amount of tomatoes in one day. Lakshmi retorted that her daughter was not going to be married to old age, brute strength, or to a budding gift for market gardening. The deadlock seemed unbreakable until Nalini suggested that he who had made the longest journey should be permitted to see her first.

It happened to be Viswakarman, who had arrived the previous night. He had come a long way and lost some of himself in the process. His face had the frightened, unnaturally brilliant look of one who by some weird negligence had been in his suit when it was sent to the cleaners. He stared at Nalini with a cautious, curious insolence. It was always better to be firm with the unknown.

'You are,' he inquired, 'no doubt a capable hussif?'

He spat the word out with a precision that made her recoil.

'I detest cooking –' she began, truthfully.

He wouldn't let her add that she was good at it, anyway.

'You must not despise the dignity of labour.'

'I'll marry you,' she retorted, 'if you promise to scrub the floor.'

'The proposal of marriage is to be made by me only. And I must satisfy myself as to your qualifications. A foreign degree and a figure are not enough. I am more concerned with diligence and humility.'

'You talk like a file,' she said. 'Sideways, you happen to look like one also.'

He stood up, trying hard to be dominating.

'You are extremely ill-mannered. A Brahmin girl should strive to be like a cow. She should furnish the household with everything but impertinence.'

She slumped her shoulders delicately and looked down. He was encouraged to see the flower droop. A sense of sympathy glowed in him, mingled with satisfaction at his own sternness.

'If you condescend to marry me,' she asked, 'you'll be able, won't you, to keep us from starvation?'

He smiled reassuringly. 'I am a journalist. India is on the verge of great achievements. Vigorous pens will be needed to announce them.'

'A journalist! How unusual! How much more original than being a teacher or lawyer.'

He buttoned his coat in an effort to look successful. It

was his father's coat unfortunately and he remained some distance from the buttons.

'I am not simply a reporter but a master of style. In fact I am a master of many styles. When I was a child I wrote like Middleton Murry. I have successfully imitated all the Nobel Prize winners. I am now maturing from early to late Eliot.'

For a moment she was startled. She was back in the study, seeing herself three years ago, watching the destruction of her proudest efforts at mimicry.

'How wonderful it would be,' she suggested, 'if you were to write like yourself.'

He reared back, surprised. 'It is impossible. I am only a novice. Before I can say anything I have to master all masters.'

'Don't you ever hear the sound of your own voice?'

'Often,' he said candidly. 'I seem to hear nothing else.'

'Then why don't you use it to say what's on your own mind?'

He smiled superciliously to conceal his embarrassment. 'First I must enter into the minds of others. If something can be said by Rabindranath Tagore or Winston Churchill, then first of all, I must say it on their behalf. If not, I can speak for myself. But that is most unlikely. If Tagore had lived for ever he would undoubtedly have said everything.'

She wished she could teach him what she herself had learnt. But she obviously wasn't meant to succeed as a teacher. She tried to convince him by a different approach.

'I'd never know whom I was married to,' she said.

He brushed the objection aside. 'I will decide the personality of your literary mentor. Valmiki perhaps, or possibly Tulsidas. You have been too long in the West. From head to foot you must be totally remoulded.'

He managed to look at her intensely, without seeing her. The feat impressed her, but also annoyed her a little. His hands made distant, fluent gestures as if he were modelling some spiritual plasticine.

'Your namesake,' she said reprovingly, 'was a wonderful architect.'

He ignored the implication that he was not of the same standard.

'You have read the *Puranas*?' he said, his face brightening. 'Splendid. You may very well be the Hindu wife of the future. In your personality Western materialism can be harmoniously yoked to Eastern spirituality.'

He looked at her with eyes that were distinctly Western materialist.

'Your namesake,' she persisted, 'did have the merit of being original.'

He shook his head. 'You have not read the *Puranas* carefully enough. He invented nothing new. What he did was to put together the best existing ingredients. That is precisely my method. That is how I shall achieve journalistic renown. That is the technique I shall apply to your remoulding.'

'Apart from this remoulding business,' she asked, 'is there any reason why you should want to marry me?'

He shrugged his shoulders to imply that her tactlessness had compelled him to an indelicate revelation.

'You are no doubt in reasonably affluent circumstances.'

'It depends on what you mean,' she answered evasively.

He began to edge to the door. 'There is a misunderstanding, I take it. Your father said plainly that you were remarkably well-endowed.'

He looked dubiously at her pendant and bangles.

'I think,' she explained, 'that my father was referring to my spiritual heritage.'

Indignantly, he paused in the exit. 'You've no right to do this to me. I have been brought here under false pretences. Was it for this that I purchased a second-class ticket?'

'Oh, please,' she pleaded mockingly. 'I'll cook for you. I'll launder all your dhotis. I'll read to you every night from the *Ramayana*.'

'You haven't even enough for a very small printing press?'

'I'll cyclostyle all your copies of the Old Masters.'

'It's disgusting,' he burst out. 'When a man comes seven hundred miles he's entitled to expect a decent dowry.'

'A good wife is supposed to be a pearl beyond price.'

'I don't want a pearl,' he protested indignantly. 'All I want is a linotype machine.'

The door slammed as he left and Lakshmi, hearing the crash, came hurrying to the rescue.

'Did he tell you who his grandfather was?'

'Oh no,' said Nalini regretfully. 'I'm afraid I never even asked.'

Lakshmi wrung her hands in remonstrance.

'My precious,' she said, caressing Nalini's shoulder, 'you simply must learn to use your ten minutes properly. Not that these people are worth bothering about. They're absolute nobodies, and I can smell their nothingness. But at least they are good enough for you to practise upon.'

'Yes, Mother,' Nalini dutifully agreed. 'Family first and then finances. And then their social circle. And I must mention those whom we *don't* want to know first.'

Her mother's face glowed. 'My dear, it's a vital precaution. A man can be your misfortune for thirty years. Yet you must discover all his secrets in ten minutes. Only a woman can hope to do that, and then only if she is flawlessly trained.'

She had to check herself from instructing Nalini about the disastrous consequences of her own lack of training.

'The next one,' she said, sticking firmly to the future, 'isn't worth five minutes of your time. What can you find out from a man who doesn't even know the first thing about himself? But your father says we must treat everyone in the same way.'

She went out, her manner suggesting clearly that very different attitudes could be conveyed by the same 'treatment'.

Satyamurti came in. He had knocked so diffidently and hesitated so long outside that Nalini had to open the door for him. He looked at everything in the room except her. It was a bare room and the evasion soon had to be abandoned.

'I am impostor,' he announced, as if he were stating his name. 'I am not even here under false pretences. I am actor with nothing about which to pretend.'

'Nobody knows what he is,' she answered gently.

He tried to smile, but his face was not meant to soften even with gratitude. It was set hard and beaten back. His eyes when they were not querulous seemed only to be determined not to flinch.

'I have no business to be here,' he said. 'Of myself there is nothing to say. Of yourself there is nothing which I have the right to ask.'

He began to bow himself clumsily out of the room. She got up and impulsively put her hand on his shoulder.

'Please stay,' she asked him. 'I wouldn't want you to feel hurt.'

He stiffened as if recoiling from her kindness. His hand gripped the security of the door-knob.

'What is it that you ask of me?'

She was taken aback. 'Nothing,' she said hastily. 'I just want you to feel that I respect you for yourself.'

His mouth trembled as he tried to relax it. 'You will judge me truly,' he asked. 'You are not concerned that I have neither father or mother?'

His intensity disturbed her. Though she had been moved by nothing more than a sense of fairness, she felt herself partially responsible for his reaction. She tried to shift the situation to a less personal plane.

'You remember our legends,' she said. 'There are so many foundlings in them who are abandoned and left to float down rivers. They always turn out to be princes or heroes.'

'I am not prince,' he told her almost viciously.

'I wouldn't care if you were a pauper,' she snapped back.

It was the wrong retort. He began to stare at her. At first it was the familiar stare of the young Indian in his twenties, belligerent, defensive and insecure, the look of a mind grown up, fashioned by abstract thought, held firm by the pressure of responsibility, but frustrated, almost caged in its dealings with others. But as she looked at him the expression in his eyes became slowly simpler, purifying itself, till nothing was left but an intensity of loneliness. He wanted to be wanted and, no matter how minor her kindnesses, they could not but open that hunger to its depths. She respected him, but she began to wonder if indifference would not be less cruel to his need.

He must have seen her feelings in her face. He moved away from her with a detached mechanical stiffness, jerking himself back from the appeal and the want on which his whole personality had been momentarily focused.

'I have detained you unnecessarily,' he said dryly.

She didn't attempt to deny it. 'There's bound to be someone somewhere,' she assured him, the trite words sounding like a reproof of her hesitations.

By now he had retreated into normality. The desire to touch others with himself had subsided. He had flinched away from the expectation of being valued and needed and his eyes recognised that he should never have nourished that hope. He held his hand out distantly, correctly, like a child at its first party following its parents' instructions.

'You've been extremely kind to me,' he said.

She put her hand gently in his, feeling his withdrawal even in his fingers. 'I believe in you,' she insisted vainly. 'It doesn't matter where you come from or who your parents are.'

He took his hand back firmly. 'For graciousness, many

thanks. And apologies for disturbance. Each man must travel own road by himself.'

When he left he almost stumbled over Lakshmi, who had been chafing and seething up and down the corridor.

'We're being mean to him,' Nalini protested when he was out of earshot. 'He's decent and serious. Why can't *we* be decent and judge him on his merits?'

'You never marry only a man,' said Lakshmi.

'I don't propose to marry anything else.'

'You're in love with him,' she wailed. Consternation leaped into her eyes. 'How can you possibly do it? With a nose like that and without even a horoscope?'

'All I want is to be fair to him.'

Lakshmi sniffed contemptuously. 'You're like your father, wanting to befriend every stray dog. Be careful or one day you'll be sorry. Today, you only want to stroke his head. Tomorrow, you'll be eating out of his begging bowl. A girl can be ruined by pity. To stay alive in India you have to harden your heart.'

'I can look after myself,' declared Nalini warmly.

'Then do that and don't go mothering others. You're meant for better things. Always ignore what can't do you any good.'

She stalked off, trying to dismiss the whole affair with her bearing. After all, Nalini was only sorry for the man and that was an emotion that common sense usually rubbed off. It was youthful sentimentality. People back from abroad were always generous to beggars until they realised that the beggars were too numerous.

When she had left Gopal sidled round the corner. In the

commotion caused by Nalini's homecoming and the inter-mittent arrival of suitors from distant places he hadn't been able to do more than look at his sister. He had wanted to watch her unpack, since suitcases from abroad were certain to contain illicit and startling secrets, but his mother kept the door closed to him, being afraid that he would see more than he should.

'You haven't brought me any comics, have you?' he asked.

'I've got you something that's even more exciting.'

His eyes lit up. 'Not murders? Gory, spine-tingling murders? The Great Detective drowning like a rat in the monsoon? Or the Case of the Cobra in the Ambassador's Baggage?'

'They're hidden away safely among my saris,' she said. 'But, Gopal, you must learn to do without them. You're much too grown up now to want to read such stuff.'

'Very well,' he said, his lips trembling. 'If you're going to be like the rest of them . . .'

The tears were starting to his eyes and she had to restrain them. In front of his parents he would stand with a stiff fortitude, never losing his temper or even raising his voice, giving them the shell of the person they had half disowned. But with her he cried easily, since he needed no pretences.

'I brought them for you, after all,' she said. 'So read them, but not too much. And don't forget the other books you're supposed to be reading.'

She winced a little at the thought of the other books, ugly, edifying and covered in brown paper. On his ninth birth-day someone had given him a train and he had watched it

with a child's absorption, imprisoned like himself, career-
ing dizzily round a circular track no bigger than a wash-
basin, until its momentum threw it off the rails. His father
had seen the elation in his face and exchanged the toy for
a text-book on geology.

'I've been told I must do nothing else but learn,' he said.
'I'm slower than the rest, so I've got to work twice as hard.
And even then father thinks I'll never learn enough.'

When he was ten they had increased his pay and for a
while he was contented, jingling the eight anna coins in his
pocket and thinking of the happiness he had embalmed in
the bright silver. Then the *Young People's Clarion* arrived
and his father, who had taken out the subscription, told him
that he would have to pay the bill. It left him with less
money than he had ever had.

Now his sister was asking him where he would conceal
his secrets and, thinking of the proper hiding-place, he
laughed gently, a delicate suppressed laugh, feeling that if
he laughed louder he might end by having to pay more.

'I'll hide it in the *Young People's Clarion*. You haven't
seen the *Young People's Clarion,* have you?'

She smiled and shook her head. 'Father must have discovered it after I left England.'

'It's more instructive than any other periodical of com-
parable price addressed to a juvenile audience. At least that's
what father says. I hope I'm repeating it right.'

It sounded grimly authentic. She felt a stab of sorrow for
him, serious, handicapped, destroying himself to fight his
way into knowledge, and a twist of anger against a tradition that never forgave failure and seldom rewarded success.

'I'll give you two of the magazines right away,' she promised.

Before she could do so Lakshmi clattered back. She glared at Gopal and drove him back to his slate. Lunch was impending, she announced, with an air that suggested that other cataclysms were now of minor importance.

Nalini helped her with the preparations. Her mother was a good cook. She had acquired the talent in her days of drudgery and consoled herself with it in her years of frustrated promise. The family always ate well, enabling Sambasivan to inform them that the mind needed to be nourished as well as the body. His views on education were comprehensive, but he was aware only of the physical aspects of neglect. His children were well cared for if they drank more milk than others.

Lakshmi cooked intuitively, not by the clock or by measures, but sniffing fastidiously as she mixed in the spices, judging everything by the emergence of the one, true aroma. Unlike many cooks, she had always been generous in enjoying her own work. Her merits as a chef had steadily increased her waistline and given her yet another misfortune to lament.

The day's meal was more elaborate than usual because she wanted to prove that the ladies of the family were able to triumph over adverse circumstances and that they were blessed with a will to civilisation which could not be extinguished even by the downpours of Mudalur. The plantain leaves were piled high with succulences, the *poppadams* were feathery light and the *thoshais* butter-soft beneath their golden crusts. Unexpectedly, Lakshmi had wanted to do the serving. Yesterday she had frozen her guests with contempt. Today she was in the mood to kill them with kindness. The family's manners had to be so instinctive, its breeding so ingrained that its equilibrium could not be disturbed even by rank outsiders and verminous upstarts. She bustled about her work, dispensing the portions with relentless and experienced generosity. As the first handful fell on each leaf, each guest would begin his crescendo of protest rising into agonised importunities and accompanied by much wringing of hands, carefully arranged so as not to hinder the serving. Lakshmi would continue until the lament tailed off into that desperate resignation which was the signal that another two spoonfuls needed to be added. When the guest had approximately what he expected he would complain piteously that it was Lakshmi's intention to make him die of over-eating. Lakshmi would retort that never in her life had she known anyone to eat so little and add that the miserable portion she had dispensed was the minimum necessary to keep ascetics from starvation. There-upon the guests would finish the food off and tune their voices to bewail the second helping.   *9 5 6 5 2*

To judge by the lamentations that were produced the sweets must have been the climax of the afternoon. The *ladoos* in particular inspired Sambasivan to observe that a good wife exceeded them in sweetness even as the cause exceeded the effect. Unfortunately his remarks were addressed to an audience not of philosophers but of *gourmands* and Lakshmi, whose figure was not wholly dissimilar to a *ladoo,* rewarded him with an unsympathetic glare. He was relieved when the coffee was served in silver tumblers. It was grown on the estate, he pointed out proudly, omitting to add that the guests were about to consume a whole year's produce.

The meal over, Lakshmi was anxious to press on with the interviews. She had been more hospitable than was necessary, and it was time to conclude the affair and to send her guests packing. The response to the advertisement had inflamed her expectations. If this was the reaction in Mudalur, what could it not be in a popular place like Madura, given a text which was less insanely drafted and which emphasised more specifically the qualities of her daughter? Instead of five applicants there would be five thousand; and instead of a collection of frustrated freaks there would be normal men with more than normally prosperous fathers. As she thought of the seething mob of suitors breaking down the iron gates of her rented house, of the extra trains that would have to be run in to Madura, and of the police constables on their stampeding horses, mopping their brows and pleading for transfer to Trichy, the conviction burned and leaped in Lakshmi's heart that this was the only way to spend a vacation. It was enough to atone for thirty-two wasted years. She was eager to redeem everything, to abandon her past to the mud, to hasten down to civilisation and the rose dust of the plains. But Sambasivan struck one of his infuriating postures. He was the sustenance of Mudalur, he declared. It ill behoved him to let his people down. He was their salvation, the root of their prosperity and the *Asoka* tree that blossomed over their heads. He would not deviate from his responsibilities even to marry his priceless pearl of a daughter. Making this proclamation gave him a gratifying sense of moral dignity and mentally added inches to his height. By declaring his daughter to be priceless, he had made the tasks of duty even more onerous, and thereby increased his own nobility in performing them. Lakshmi reasoned with him for nearly five minutes and then up-braided him for an hour and a half. Sambasivan mounted the black stone plinth in front of the sundial, partly in self-defence, but also to deliver a three-hour sermon on silence as the most eminent of womanly virtues. This he would undoubtedly have done if the rain had not catastrophically intervened. By then it was becoming dark and the lightning put on a display that was truly fearsome. It was an evil omen, everyone agreed. The heavens were obviously warning someone, but each felt that the other was the culprit. At any rate, there was no point in going anywhere except into the innermost depths of Hillview.

While the rain lashed at the windows, the night swooped down in a crushing envelopment that stifled every star. It lay on one's thoughts with a demanding weight of emptiness. One tried to force one's mind away from its questionings only to be drawn more surely into its depths. Nalini opened her eyes against the vaguely singing darkness, through which the rain beat in the irregular drumming of a memory, a fear pushing its way into the senses that would not receive it. Had she come home only to the trap of growing old? There were many roads to emptiness, but they all began at the sacred fire of marriage when the bridegroom was dissuaded from his journey to Benares only to lead the bride to a different death. She thought of the different ways of extinction, of the way of duty, of drudgery upheld with pride and fortitude till the house filled gradually with children and one could ebb away into the strength of their growth. Then there was the more prosperous form of dying, devouring *jilabis* and screaming at many servants, till the thickening waistline turned one to the penance of social work and the stab of pain let in the light of religion. There was the imported alternative of romantic love. She snuggled up to the thought, trying to swoon in front of it, but the night took it and wound it around her instead, making it only into a pleasant suffocation. The morning would come and the death could not be repeated. Satyamurti's face implored her from the shadows, the eyes flinching back, the nose thrusting forward like a defensive rampart. Should she pity him, pour her generosity into him, drive him into a frenzy of achievement? She pricked a pin into the darkness and pulled out a voice from the crowd. It was the nine hundred and eleventh answer to her marriage advertisement. A voice unattached to a person. She would see the face only on the night of her wedding, not the eyes she would look into during the ceremony itself, but the other face after the presents had been put away and the shy student had turned into the caged animal. She might yoke herself, she thought, to any body and the excess of the first moments, whether love or disgust, would subside eventually into the same resignation. But she herself would be intact. However much given, she would remain apart.

Almost angrily she brushed away the fascination of those thoughts that lay so close to her lips. The night seemed to be in her lungs now, so that in fighting it off she shared its darkness. She could make the pattern, she reminded herself, and not simply preserve her identity in it. She could choose her own life and not simply choose her smile when she looked up into the doomed, demanding face, forsaken and avid, of the life that was given. She spoke her convictions gently to the night and in her imagination the hills held it, reminding her how they, too, had been softened into submission by the everlasting tryst of cloud and rain.

Where was she to find the appropriate fate, the right incompleteness to welcome, to cherish into the other half of her image? By advertisement, by the conjunction of stars, or by the right combination of pedigree and performance? Would she find the inclusive formula in the exclusive club, mixing inferior Scotch with apish English, the hollow man with the obsequious voice who in five years' time would be suddenly stuffed with Indianness? Should she choose the patriot who had suffered for the dream and seen it realised and who now accepted the benefits of freedom from the same brown masters who had once put him in jail? Perhaps she should not marry at all but join the Foreign Service, where every ambassador's brief-case would be her handbag.

Her forebodings slithered away as the dawn broke open the night, washing out the emptiness while the rain struck at her mind in the monotonous, consoling drumming of normality. She unglued her eyelids and opened her thoughts reluctantly to the day's dazzlings. When the water slapped at her face, the sleepiness scaled off, but there were faint lights of rebellion which she could not extinguish. She tried to make her discontent more precise, picturing herself reproachfully descending a majestic marble stairway, while those who were guilty huddled at the foot of it, waiting for her judgment. In fact she stumbled out of her circle, disconcerted to find her parents at her feet, pouring coffee in and out of brass tumblers. She had had enough of interviews, she said; in her resentment she was certain at least of that. A girl had the right to make up her own mind, she added, the words following almost automatically and sounding absurd as soon as they were detached from her.

'But of course, you're free,' said Sambasivan, puzzled. 'You can choose anyone who is fit to be chosen.'

'There'll be at least two thousand of them,' promised Lakshmi. 'The marriage season begins in April, so that comes to six every day for the next ten months, excluding Deepavali and Tamil New Year. So why grumble about a mere three people yesterday? You're out of condition, that's what you are, poor girl. You've lived too long among labour-saving gadgets.'

Nalini subsided delicately on to her plank, simmering over the coffee which her mother offered her.

'It's immoral,' she protested, 'to interview people whom you have no intention of marrying.'

'What's immoral about trying to get your eye in? They came here of their own free will, didn't they? So you can't argue that they don't deserve it. Besides, they've eaten enough to make themselves useful.'

'Nalini's ideas are different now,' Sambasivan proclaimed. He was ponderous even in his teasing. 'She believes in true love like a gong in the heart. Somewhere in India her soul-mate awaits her. He reads no advertisements. He can be found only by the eternal pilgrim.'

'How ravishing,' chortled Lakshmi. 'Do tell me all about

him, Nalini dear! Is he like one of our ancient epic heroes, tall as a *Sala* tree, with eyes red at the corners and long arms like snakes? Is his skin like beaten gold or melted butter? Do tell me so that I can find something superior.'

'He's an artist,' said Sambasivan. 'One of those emancipated chaps. With an inherited house and a hired clique to applaud him. He falls in and out of love between the courses of a fifty-course dinner. He's suffered so little for his convictions that he's lost them.'

Nalini sipped her coffee and smiled back. It was the best face she could put on her discomfiture. They were too fond of her to be overbearing, but the bantering pin-pricks were meant to make it clear that happiness lay only in intelligent submissiveness (reconciliation, they would have preferred to call it), and that to dream of escaping was only childish petulance. She found herself stiffened instinctively by the thought. If that was her fate she would let her fate flow over her. There was a flame of personality that could not be extinguished.

What was the point of having been in the West, she wondered. One came back eventually to the sacrifice. Year after year millions of people like her, with henna-red feet and garments of gold tissue, would circle devoutly the flame and ordeal of marriage. Little by little the storm would break one open. The procession of clouds across the greying hills would flood dispassionately into one's mind, pushing it down into annihilation, quietening it insistently into its final darkness. One kept one's identity, maintained one's defences, and if one was well taught the struggle was only longer, the pain of acceptance more drawn out and acute.

Her hands reached out and she had to take them back hurriedly, realising that she was warming herself in front of an imaginary fire. She sensed that her smile was unaltered. Her feelings had already learned how to retreat from her face.

She shrugged her shoulders and the mood disappeared. It was no more than that, only a passing sombreness. But it slipped into her feelings unannounced, pervading them with the slow rot of its colour, and the time might come when it would no longer be foreign.

'I'm ready,' she said, with a gaiety meant partly to re-assure herself. 'Ready to go on with the show.'

'Don't take it seriously,' Lakshmi advised her. 'That's what's tiring you out. Live away from your skin, it's the secret of all happiness.'

Nalini went to the room where the interviews were held. There was a picture of Saraswathi on the wall, cow-eyed and expressionless on a rock in the forest. She bowed to it slightly in her heart, telling herself that no one ever stopped learning. In front of her was a curtain of soiled lace. When the candidate had entered and sat down with his back to it, she was supposed to glide in demurely through its folds. She amused herself by practising various entries. How precisely would she steal upon his senses? With the hesitant cough, the carefully exaggerated rustle of bangles and silks, or with the lilting voice like clear spring water, delightfully offering him a glass of fruit juice? She would stand at the window, unconscious of his presence, looking out at her dreams, bedraggled like the zinnias. Then she would turn around, impelled by an unseen force and with a cry of ardour, hurl herself at her destiny.

'Excellent indeed!' the mellow voice said. 'The back view is decidedly auspicious.'

She whirled rather than turned around, so disconcerted that she forgot even her *namaskar*. 'How dare you speak to me like that,' she chided him hotly.

He was of medium height and stockily built. He had a sleek skin, ceremoniously oiled. His dhoti was of the very best silk, his white shirt expensively homespun, and his plain slippers made of butter-soft leather that would have done credit to the most select of ladies' handbags. He was dressed to an image of dignified frugality that must have cost him a minor fortune to imitate.

'Excellent,' he repeated, unperturbed. 'You have dulcet tones to add to a classical figure. It seems probable that you can bless a household with good fortune.'

'Who on earth do you think you're supposed to be?' she demanded.

'No one on earth,' he corrected her. 'I am named after Kubera, god of riches.'

'I suppose you're disgustingly wealthy like your name-sake.'

He patted his chest complacently. 'Let us say that I am not entirely without means.'

'Money isn't a substitute for manners.' She reproved herself at once for having said that. But there was something about the man that made her sententious.

He looked at her approvingly. 'Your anger, too, is excellent. I expect my future wife to be a woman of spirit. In principle I find you satisfactory. Consequently let us get

down to business. You are related to the Nellora Naray-
anans?'

'I've never had anything to do with them.'

'Indeed. That is unfortunate. In that case perhaps the
Vellore Vaidyanabhans?'

'I've never known anyone whom you could possibly
meet.'

'Excellent,' he beamed. 'A lady without liabilities. If
you've no relatives so much the better. I shan't have to
pay for their upkeep and for idiot sons who can't take college
degrees. I'm completely against this dowry, pedigree business. My policy has always been to take people on their
merits. Character and substance are what I demand in my
consort.'

'That's liberal of you,' she said. 'I simply can't stand you,
so I'd love to know what I am throwing out.'

'That is a question which always answers itself.'

He looked at her in a way that compelled her to look back.
He was several years older than herself, a man who had
beaten his own road through life and then smoothed the
consequences carefully out of his skin. His face was square,
his expression impassive and confident, withdrawn and
dominating, a nice combination of the bludgeon and the
Buddha. She was haunted by that face. She hadn't just
seen it before. She felt she had always been seeing it. And
yet she couldn't remember to whom the face belonged.

'Don't be disturbed,' he said. 'You think you have met
me already. You have, and so have tens of thousands of
others.'

'You're not a politician?' she inquired desperately.

He flicked the unseemly question off his shirt. 'Obviously not. I am a man of taste. But some politicians owe their well-being to me.'

'Then you must be a financier.'

'My dear girl, what is the point of this catechism? You remember me because you cannot avoid me. You've always known me because you're destined to share life with me.' He rose from his seat and moved forward purposefully. She backed into a corner, her eyes blazing.

'If you dare to touch me, I'll scream.'

He was genuinely surprised. 'Why should I need to touch you? There is a certain decorum in these matters. Apparently you've forgotten that in America.'

'I detest you. I stamp on the thought of marrying you.'

'I approve of you and your family will approve of me. The rest does not matter. Your hostilities will dissolve in our identity of interests. You are everything I have looked for in a wife. Sophisticated and yet unspoilt. Vivid and yet not blatant. Your figure can do justice to the finest of silks. Your skin is softer than the most exquisite powder. Your magnificent eyes would market oceans of lotions. And your hair! What can one say of your hair? It is your benediction, the very richness of darkness –'

'I know you now,' she cried out, her eyes widening. 'I know where I've seen you, why I can't forget. It isn't true, tell me it isn't true.'

She sank dizzily into the nearest chair. He produced a bottle of smelling-salts and waved it under her nose. She pushed it away, angrily.

'Must you even have your wretched picture on that?'

'The world is unscrupulous. One has to protect one's followers.'

'I should have guessed it,' she said. 'There was something about your face; familiar and inevitable. It's been staring at me every day from my dressing-table.'

'On which bottle, may I ask?'

'Why, the large green one in which you are tap-dancing on the head of a cobra.'

'I knew it,' he cried happily. 'Kubera's Cosmic Cream. I knew I was responsible for something in your beauty. From the moment I came into this room I had that faint, unmistakable feeling of achievement. Without Kubera such hair could not exist. With me it can call to every woman from every dressing-table through the length and breadth of India, Pakistan, Ceylon and Madagascar. Not just as a dream, but as a living possibility, a sleek, velvety, glowing loveliness of darkness.'

'You talk like a television advertisement,' she said.

'Television, bah! A primitive form of publicity. On television you can appear for a maximum of two minutes. You have to compete with baseball games and symphony orchestras. On my bottles you will forever beckon to my clients always inescapably, at the time of maximum impact. They can never forget you. You will live in their thoughts and sink into their psyches. You will be etched on their imaginations in envy and in hope. I shall make you a cosmetic myth, a status symbol.'

She shuddered at the thought of her greasy future and he pressed on, enraptured by his argument.

'It is not a matter of your hair alone. Cosmic Cosmetics

is an expanding, forward-looking organisation, progressive, virile, imaginative and dynamic. We are equipped to exploit all aspects of your beauty. I can see the whole programme before me. I shall create a new perfume entirely in your honour. A wedding present. You will be drenched in its seduction. Attar of Darkness. You must make the name famous. Tell them you have been to America, Europe, Fifth Avenue, the Faubourg St Germain. You have tried Lanvin, Curvel, Balenciaga, Schiaparelli. Nothing, but nothing, compares with Attar of Darkness, the Prime Minister of Perfumes, exquisitely nationalist, quintessentially Indian, made rigorously to a sacred, secret formula older than history, newer than nuclear physics.'

'You won't catch me living up to that,' said Nalini.

'You will marry me,' he insisted. 'Some women achieve greatness. Others have greatness sprayed upon them.'

'There's one thing I can't understand,' she said. 'You are successful and you must be sought after. You simply aren't the type that answers advertisements.'

'It wasn't the advertisement that brought me here.'

'Then what did? This isn't a thriving market for cosmetics.'

'As I said before, we believe in the forward tack. Cosmic Cosmetics must diversify its interests. If I become too prosperous I am likely to be nationalised. Consequently I am on the alert for new fields to conquer.'

'Well, you won't do much conquering in whatever fields we've got here. Rice, fruit, a small amount of coffee. That's what we grow, and I doubt if it'll do you good.'

'You are certain that is all?'

'What else can there possibly be to interest you?'

'There are legends, are there not, of a sacred plant that grows here?'

'Of course,' she cried. 'You mean the mangoes of Mudalur.'

His eyes shone with a passion he had not shown in admiring her.

'You have heard of them?' he demanded. 'You are able to lead me to them?'

She took him to the window. The clouds had withdrawn from their battle with the peak itself but had surged over its shoulders so that the summit seemed to float, detached and inaccessible, against the green-grey masses. The air had that startling, purged lucidity, only possible in the intervals between downpours. It had cleansed the peak of every nuance and distraction of light, making it stand forth in a clear and shapely monotony, a claim and a confession from which she could not withdraw. She turned to him, watching the effect upon him. He, too, seemed lost in reverie as he scanned the tall cliffs with the clouds scudding across them.

'It's an ugly proposition, isn't it?' he said.

'How can you!' she burst out. 'I think it's serene and beautiful.'

'Not to the person who has to climb it.'

'No one in Mudalur has. They love it too much.'

'Then how do they know that the tree up there is holy?'

'How could any tree possibly grow there if it wasn't? And besides, a *rishi* lived under it for eight years.'

'And how precisely is he supposed to have got there?'

'That's another proof of holiness.'

'Is that all the proof there is?' His voice sounded disappointed. 'You are unable to provide me with more satisfactory evidence?'

'Well, a long time ago there was a great storm and many of the mangoes blew down. Some were found at the foot of the cliff. Strange to say, they were more or less undamaged. A lame man ate one and was able to walk again. A woman who was childless had two sons.'

'Splendid. This is far more credible. From the publicity viewpoint, I mean. The tale is, of course, fully authenticated?'

'Why, everybody in the village believes it.'

'Excellent. That is preferable even to its being true.'

'But it's never happened after that,' she said. 'The mangoes always fall and rot at the summit. It needs a tremendous wind to blow them down here.'

'And no one has ever gone up to the top? Even though they know that the fruit is miraculous?'

'I don't think it ever occurred to them. It's a question of respect for something holy.'

'Rubbish,' he scoffed. 'It's the national style of living: to sit with mouths open waiting for mangoes to fall in them. Well, Cosmic Cosmetics will soon put an end to that. How long do you say it is since this great event occurred?'

'It's odd that you should ask that,' she said. 'As a matter of fact, it was exactly fifty monsoons ago.'

He clapped his hands. 'An excellent coincidence. This will be a year of miracles. The mountain will be climbed and the tree's harvest gathered. It will be eaten at a great festival, possibly on the night of your wedding. That will provide a double-barrelled *tamasha*. If the *tamasha* is adequate the results will certainly follow. Those who suffer misfortune will immediately blame the government. Those who have the sons they were going to have or pass the examinations they were going to pass will hasten to credit the fruit with supernatural properties. If people are slow in believing, the *tamasha* can be intensified. Blind men can be imported into Mudalur; fortunately there are none in the village. They will eat the fruit, recover the perfect vision which they always possessed and loudly proclaim the fruit's miraculous virtues. If necessary, a leper can take part in the scheme of persuasion. He will be given Sulfone treatment and a teaspoonful of mango juice every evening. After six weeks he will recover – I shall take care to select him on that basis. The treatment will be forgotten and the mangoes revered.'

'You're disgusting,' she said angrily. 'I knew there was something mean about you from the beginning. A toad living on the superstitions of others.'

He stiffened a little. 'Be good enough to think before you judge. I shall refrain scrupulously from making any claim whatever. The people will draw their own conclusions. If they want to believe in miraculous mangoes, let them. Who am I to interfere? It is their democratic right.'

'It's indecent,' she said. 'You're abusing the faith of those simple villagers. You're treating them like fools. You're taking away their self-respect. If that isn't contemptible I'd like to know what is.'

'Taking away their self-respect? On the contrary, that's

exactly what I'm giving them. A whole grove will be planted from those mango seeds. Mudalur will become a place of pilgrimage. Rest-houses can be built, not too well equipped – a little discomfort helps the feeling of holiness. The road up here can be widened and properly surfaced. New implements and fertilisers can be bought. People won't just sit and dream of the wind rising. They will work with energy and a sense of their future. Does it matter if an illusion makes them work? Will you tell me then that the mangoes are a legend?'

He paced by the window, his expression almost hostile as he looked at the peak.

'On what day was the storm?' he asked.

'On the night of the full moon. That would be four nights from now.'

'Then it must be climbed on that day.'

'The monsoon makes it twice as dangerous.'

His fingers drummed impatiently against the window. 'I am used to overcoming obstacles. If one is to succeed, risks must be taken.'

'I can't agree with your arguments,' she said. 'To be honest, I detest them. But I respect your courage.'

'Courage?' he asked, puzzled. 'I don't see where that comes into it.'

She was pleasantly surprised. She hadn't expected modesty in him.

'It takes courage to climb that cliff. Particularly for you. You can't know very much about the business of climbing.'

'Don't be absurd!' he said. 'Do you seriously think that the man you are going to marry, on whom you depend to make you famous all over India, on whom the whole future of this village rests, is going to risk his life and that of the vital issues that depend upon it by clambering up a cliff-face like a demented baboon? Other people will do it, if the reward is suitable. There will be an expedition, but I shall not be physically part of it. I shall direct the proceedings from my future father-in-law's telescope.'

'I hate you,' she almost screamed. 'Get out of the room before I throw something at you.'

'Excellent,' he said, indomitably. 'It is better for a marriage to begin in anger than to end in sorrow.'

He left the room, smiling. She was too furious to do a *nanashar,* but he acknowledged the courtesy even though it was not there. Kalyanasundaram came in, attracted by the commotion.

'Wonderful collection of cranks and coots,' he said. 'Please tell me of your reaction to them.'

'What business is it of yours?' she demanded icily.

'Oh dear! Oh dear! That Arctic Circle voice again. Far be it from me to probe your delicate feelings. It's just to provide material for my book.'

'As far as I am concerned, you can throw your precious book into the waste-paper-basket.'

'I thought you were a friend of mine,' he reproached her. 'You never told me that you were a literary critic.'

'Can't you think of anything but your obnoxious manuscript?'

'Women should admire men who are single-minded.'

He tried to look masterful and she burst out laughing. He winced and then began to smile also.

'These people,' she said, 'have come an awfully long way. Whatever their motives, one must respect their feelings.'

'I wouldn't dream of doing otherwise. Whatever you say will be strictly confidential. No names whatever will be mentioned in my book. They will be mere threads in a pattern of degeneracy.'

'You're disgustingly callous.'

'You're impossibly vain.'

'You think of everyone as material for your book.'

'And you think of them as suitors at your *swayamvara*. Two years in a kitchen might teach you some humility.'

'I won't be as mean as that,' she retorted. 'All I wish you is two nights on that mountain.'

'Under the famous mango tree undoubtedly. Seriously, have you ever heard such nonsense? Men seeing again and all that kind of drivel!'

She wanted to disagree violently with him. She had to remind herself of her Western education.

'It might help you to write better,' she suggested.

'Rubbish. You're not saying it because of concern for my style. You want me to get you a mango, that's why. It's your Western education. You won't look at a man till he brings you the Golden Fleece.'

'How utterly ridiculous!'

'It's the truth, isn't it?'

'Is isn't, but any of the other men would do it.'

'The more fools they,' he snorted. 'In India it's the women who are supposed to go through ordeals.'

He made for the door and she opened it with alacrity.

'I'll bring you a mango,' he promised. 'An ordinary,

luscious mango from the market. It won't bring you holiness, but it'll teach you common sense.'

When he had left she went to the window. The light had forced itself through the cloudbanks, softening them into an iron grey. Its rays struggled towards the peak, silvering it slightly, giving it a quality which was less radiance than a pensive, soothing coldness. Its shape was withdrawn, self-contained, a concentration of solitude. Her eyes moved inevitably to the apex, sensing in it not a climax of defiance, but a compelling and consoling repose. Yet it was repose made possible only by resistance. Perhaps there was no other equilibrium, no promise more fruitful than that of rain and rock. The summit struck upwards, proclaiming her own personality, appealing, unyielding, in its stripped power of loneliness. Perhaps the only marriage that she coveted was marriage into the deep night of that power.

3

Seventy-five Per Cent Wettable

IT WAS IMPOSSIBLE to understand how the jeep had arrived. It stood there travel-rusted and significantly absurd, like a stocking waving from the top of the town hall or a bicycle hung from the spire of a college chapel. The man who had driven it and whom the villagers had already begun to compare to the legendary charioteer Nala, was obviously the victim of his talent, propelled by it into achieving the impossible and the useless. This fact made him potentially holy since he was evidently devoted to action rather than to its fruits. He was tall and pleasantly loose-limbed with an intelligently ugly face, knocked into shape by every one else's objections. He had a sensitive mouth and a combative jaw. His blue eyes flickered with the root and branch look, softened in its reforming ardour by the hydra-headed jungle of India's life.

He stamped his feet, whirled his arms and stood forebodingly in his mud-stained puttees, demanding and critical, a question-mark of change. His shirt was half out of his trousers; in its palmier days it might have been mistaken for a dish-rag. He must have been fair in his innocence; but under the avid sun his skin had blazed into the roast-beef radiance dreamed of by every mosquito. He walked towards the sandalwood house with the springy, purposeful stride of a man who never looked backwards and who believed that antibiotics could conquer every evil. The villagers gave way to him cautiously on either side, uncertain whether he was religious or insane. At the entrance to the drive he turned round and surveyed them.

'Is this place Muddle Ore?' he demanded accusingly.

The local population hung their heads in shame.

'Who's in charge around here?'

'I am,' said Sambasivan, who had come to the gate. 'That is to say, I am not unconnected with the administration of this place.'

The stranger held out his hand in a pioneering gesture.

'I'm from the malaria team,' he announced. 'My name's Ernest,' he added, without a trace of irony.

Sambasivan looked dubiously at him.

'You haven't come in answer to the advertisement, have you?'

Ernest's tone was reproving. 'I never read advertisements. My function in life is to make people healthier.'

He rolled his sleeve back over a functional forearm.

'I'm afraid you won't find much to do here,' Sambasivan apologised. 'We're really quite a small place. And besides, we're a little too high for malaria.'

'How many cases have been reported in this neighbourhood?'

'Nothing's been reported. We don't have that kind of

system. But there may have been a few cases here and there.'

'Precisely how many do you mean by a few?'

'My dear man!' protested Sambasivan mildly. 'Why talk to me as if I were an authority on the subject? I only come here for my vacations, you know. But off-hand, I'd say there were fifteen to twenty.'

'And the population of Mudalur is about three hundred?'

'Two hundred and ninety-nine to be precise. There's a new arrival called Raman. Infernal nuisance. Much worse than malaria.'

Ernest ignored the attempted diversion.

'In other words,' he insisted, 'you have a six per cent incidence.'

'If you put it that way, it does sound rather a bad show.'

'It's more than bad, it's disgraceful. Mobile H.Q. ought to have known about this.'

'Well, no one, mobile or otherwise, ever asked. No reason why they should either. We're tucked away here rather cleverly, you know. As a matter of fact, we aren't on most maps.'

'Mosquitoes don't read maps,' said Ernest glumly.

A gleam of hope straggled into his eyes.

'How far away did you say we were from anywhere?'

'I never said anything about distances. But, if you want to know, Arkayam is the nearest inhabited place.'

'Oh yes, Arkayam,' Ernest said, remembering it gloomily. 'Six miles probably, as the mosquito flies. It's well within the operational radius of the insect.'

He squared his shoulders and confronted his problem.

'Thank goodness it isn't too big a job. Sixty mud huts or thereabouts. That wouldn't be more than three thousand square yards of surface. I've got enough seventy-five per cent wettable to do the thing twice over.'

He stared at the pagoda shape of Hillview, as if by looking at it he could squash it down further.

'You realise that your place must be sprayed too?'

'By all means, my dear fellow. We'll all bathe in your wettable if it makes you feel more secure. But first come in and have a cup of tea. It's the authentic stuff, you know. Grown next door and then imported from England. Meanwhile you must meet the other members of my family. If my eyes do not deceive me, my daughter Nalini is about to join us.'

His eyes had not deceived him, though he soon wished they had. Nalini came out on the veranda, eyed the scene first with curiosity, then with amazement, and then threw out her hands in a gesture of exhilaration and ran down the drive, her eyes brimming with happiness.

'It's Ernest,' she cried. 'You of all people! Here of all places! How perfectly wonderful of you to come to see us, Ernest! How's Jim? And John? And Joan— And the Royal Doulton— Has Elizabeth taken her doctorate? Is she really marrying that windbag from Detroit?'

'You know this person?' Sambasivan inquired, with masterful logic.

'Know him! How could I ever forget him? He's been my very best friend ever since we both fell into Lake Placid.'

'Placid, indeed!' a threatening voice boomed. 'I see

absolutely nothing to be placid about.' Everyone stopped
to look at Lakshmi, who advanced magisterially to the
centre of the stage and stood with her arms raised like a
traffic constable trying to arrest the stream of terrible
thoughts.

'Who is this man?' she demanded of the universe.

'I guess you're Nell's mother,' Ernest said.

'Nell!' snorted Lakshmi. 'What makes you think I know
anyone called Nell? Are you under the impression that this
place is Covent Garden? Do I look to you like the wife of
a vegetable vendor?'

'Mother, I'm Nell,' Nalini explained. 'All my friends in
Columbia called me that.'

'Your friends! You were foolish enough to have friends
in America? And you dare to tell me that this character is
one of them?'

'Hang it all,' her husband protested. 'I know we told
Nalini to be careful, but you can't study in America without meeting some Americans. It's one of the peculiar things
about the country.'

'You keep out of this,' snapped Lakshmi. 'It's your folly
that led to this disaster. It's you who brought this nemesis
like a boomerang upon us.'

She turned peremptorily to Ernest. 'Young man, precisely
what is your purpose in coming here?'

'I'm a public health man,' said Ernest.

'My God!' said Lakshmi. 'Is it as serious as all that?'

'Six per cent of the people in Mudalur are affected.'

'How dare you!' said Lakshmi, indignantly. 'Nalini only
arrived three days ago.'

'You misunderstand him,' Sambasivan explained. 'He's talking about wiping out mosquitoes.'

'You're quite wrong there,' Ernest said eagerly. He was relieved to change the subject. 'That's the pre-war theory of malaria control: elaborate, expensive and inconclusive. Modern techniques have transformed the picture, revolutionised the economics. They've made control simple, effective and within the reach of every public health budget. And it's just a question of changing the attack. You interrupt transmission instead of destroying the insect.'

He stopped, suddenly aware that none of them was listening.

'I'm being too technical,' he concluded lamely.

'You see,' said Sambasivan. 'It isn't as bad as all that. The young man is apparently wedded to his work.'

'I wouldn't count on that,' Lakshmi said gloomily.

'Oh well, we'll soon find out.' He turned to Ernest. 'You did say you hadn't answered the advertisement?'

'What was in it?' Ernest asked.

'It offers Nalini to the most suitable suitor.'

Ernest's face broke into a smile of unconcealed pleasure. 'You can say that again,' he chortled. 'That's great. That's real progressive. That's something they haven't even *thought* of doing on TV.'

'I knew it,' groaned Lakshmi. 'God has four arms and the devil has four feet.'

'What for?' asked Sambasivan.

'So that, like you, he can put them all into one mouth.'

'Sambasivan turned anxiously to Ernest. 'You realise, of course, that this offer is limited to Indians?'

124

'I realise nothing of the sort,' said Ernest. 'And, what's more, it's illegal. Let me tell you, you can't do this to me. It's discrimination. It's against the Constitution and the United Nations Charter. As an American citizen, I demand my rights.'

'Of course, of course,' said Sambasivan hastily. 'The point is not in dispute. If you insist, you must be treated on the same basis as others.'

'Sure, I insist,' said Ernest. 'From the time I set eyes on her I knew that this long-stemmed stem of a lotus was for me. That's what her name means, don't it? Stem of a lotus? Boy, what a flower it holds up.'

Sambasivan coughed warningly. 'I was hoping you would be reasonable. However, it appears that your misguided mind has been made up. In that case, we have no alternative but to proceed to the preliminaries. Can I take it that you have provided yourself with a horoscope?'

He looked at Lakshmi triumphantly. This would put the interfering foreigner in his place.

'Horoscope?' said Ernest. 'You bet your life I got one. It's my most precious document. Nell did it for me when I fished her out of Lake Placid. And it says in it definitely that we were meant for each other,'

Sambasivan's voice was less confident. 'Your family tree, I suppose, is in perfect order.'

'It's long enough to remind me that I wasn't born yesterday.'

'I see. In a way I suppose you're right. One shouldn't make too much of this ancestry business, particularly considering some of the people we've got here.'

'What happens now?' asked Ernest.

'If you're determined to do so, you can compete with the others.'

Ernest's face brightened. 'Competition! You couldn't say anything sweeter to an American. It's the spirit of competition that made my country great. And a competition with Nell as the jackpot! Brother, that's baksheesh! When does it start? Where are these other guys you were dimly hinting about? When can I begin to wipe the veranda with them?'

'Control yourself,' said Sambasivan. He turned to Lakshmi. 'We have no choice but to be hospitable to our visitor. He has come far and is apparently flushed with achievement. Perhaps the rains will dampen his ardour a little. We can only hope that common sense will prevail.'

Lakshmi glared at him grimly. 'It's much more likely that nature will take its course.'

Reluctantly she led Ernest into the house. 'It seems I cannot forbid you to sit down.'

'Thank you kindly, ma'am,' said Ernest. 'With you as my mother-in-law, I could win the next war, one-handed.'

'Is it true,' she asked sweetly, 'that you have a certain affinity for insects?'

'I make my living trying to control them.'

'Well, then you can make yourself at home here. There are many varieties of vermin in this house.'

'Ernest settled into the arm-chair and rocketed out of it with a yell of dismay. He looked around vainly for a means of assault.

'Don't worry,' said Sambasivan. 'The cobra isn't alive.

126

You see, I offer a reward for snakes killed and there's a specially high one for cobras. So the village people kept bringing the same one back. After I'd paid for it five times I took it away and made an arm-rest out of it. It's original and it reminds me not to be too trusting. I always think, don't you, that furniture should serve a didactic as well as a functional purpose. It's what you might call killing two snakes with one stone.'

Ernest nursed his arm and looked unsympathetically at the arm-rest.

'You might let me know if there are any other nasty surprises.'

'There's a stuffed crocodile in the lavatory, that's all. Helps to create the appropriate state of suspense.'

He came to the conclusion that his visitor didn't approve of his philosophy of house furnishing.

'Spectacular journey you made here,' he said, changing the subject. 'And the rains have been the worst in living memory. I shouldn't have thought a jeep could ever do it.'

'Well, here I am,' said Ernest unnecessarily.

'If you came up,' said Lakshmi, 'the others can go down. And it's about time they did too. They've eaten too much and over-stayed their welcome. And they've seen her six times as often as they should.'

'It can't be done,' said Ernest.

Lakshmi's face coloured. 'You haven't even seen them, and yet you take their side.'

'Nobody can get down now,' Ernest explained. 'The rain must have weakened the supports of the bridge. And the jeep was probably too heavy. Anyway, the whole structure cracked open, flapped in the air a bit and went down into the gorge with a tremendous crash. After I'd got over, of course, I filmed it all on the Rolex. In Kodachrome too. Mobile H.Q. is going to have plenty to brood about.'

There was a good deal of brooding outside Mobile H.Q. Ernest seemed unaware of it. He looked with gratification at the tense circle of faces.

'We're isolated,' he said. 'The mosquitoes aren't but we are. I've said it before, and now it's been proved to the hilt. A mass health programme depends on communications.'

He became aware of the despondency around him.

'Cheer up,' he consoled them. 'It isn't as bad as all that. I only lost one drum of seventy-five per cent wettable.'

Lakshmi's emotions were the first to break loose.

'We're done for,' she wailed. 'I always said we'd die in this filthy place. And those ghouls of guests will dance on our dead bodies. We're marooned with them for ever in this mud-bath. They'll eat us out of house and home and hovel. And they'll ruin our daughter's delicate reputation.'

'Oh, it can't be as bad as that,' said Sambasivan, trying feebly to swim against the alliterative flood.

'I don't want your consolations,' she snapped back. 'I want a bridge built immediately over that gorge.'

Ernest shook his head and looked discouraging.

'It's a major engineering project,' he declared. 'Eighty feet across, if it's an inch. And a seven-hundred-and-nineteen-feet fall into the rapids. I worked it out with a stop-watch when the D.D.T. went down.'

'We could throw something across,' suggested Sambasivan. 'A temporary structure made of rope.'

'How much rope do you have in Mudalur?' Ernest asked.

'Seventy-eight feet,' Sambasivan admitted. 'But we could tie on one of Lakshmi's older saris.'

'And how are you going to fix the other side?' inquired Lakshmi witheringly. 'You'll souse my sari in seccotine, I suppose? Or fill it with the coconuts that ought to be thrown at your head?'

Her face brightened slightly as she thought of a partial solution.

'At least the guests can trek down through the forest. They're no better than savages, anyway. Two writers, one foundling, and a gluttonous witch-doctor. I've had enough of them, I tell you. If it is my fate to die of starvation in this wilderness, let me at least perish in a clean house.'

'But there are elephants in the forest,' Sambasivan protested. 'These people came here in answer to our advertisement. It wouldn't be sporting to pound them into the undergrowth.'

'If I were a man,' said Lakshmi, 'wild elephants wouldn't keep me from leaving Mudalur.'

Nalini coughed diplomatically.

'Perhaps we could break the bad news to our guests. They're in it with the rest of us. And one of them might have a useful suggestion.'

The guests had so far remained aloof, not because of any lack of curiosity, but because the new visitor might have arrived with the same purpose as themselves. It would have been odd for an American to answer a marriage advertisement; but odd things happened every day in Mudalur, and the American himself was something of an oddity. If he had come with marriage in view, certain basic inquiries had to be completed. Now, however, the interrogation seemed to have ended and they trooped in eagerly, anxious to learn the results.

'Ernest Hamilton Jones,' said Sambasivan, making the announcement like an ex-chief of protocol. 'Mr Jones is an anti-malaria expert.'

'Splendid to see you here,' Kalyanasundaram said. 'A Point Four man with real mud on his puttees. I've always thought of you people as holed up in Delhi, pow-wowing with bureaucrats. How interesting to find out that I am wrong.'

'It's a common misconception,' Ernest said charitably.

'That's what I'm glad to see.'

'You don't happen to be connected with public health?'

'In a sense, yes,' said Kalyan. 'My job is to safeguard areas of infection.'

'B.C.G., I suppose.'

'Well, not exactly.'

'Fertilisers, or environmental sanitation?'

'Sanitation, that's just it,' Kalyan agreed enthusiastically. 'What a wonderfully vivid way to describe my task!'

'It's public works, not public health,' said Ernest. 'But it's really a health problem. When you get down to brass tacks, it's unclean water. Ninety per cent of the man-hours lost in this country are lost through an unsafe water supply.'

'You aren't married, are you?' Kalyanasundaram asked.

Ernest frowned in perplexity.

'I don't understand what that has to do with tube-wells.'

Sambasivan cleared his throat portentously.

'A crisis is confronting us,' he announced, steering the conversation back to its main object. 'We appear to have crossed the Rubicon. We have burned our bridges or, more correctly, sunk them.'

He went on to describe the situation with more clarity.

'I'm sorry,' he added. 'You may have to stay with us a bit longer. We'll do our best to see that you're not uncomfortable.'

To his surprise, nobody seemed greatly depressed.

'I don't mind it here at all,' Kalyanasundaram said. 'I've a survey to complete, and the place is full of fascinating material. Murugesan's daughter, for instance. How on earth can he afford such a hefty dowry?'

'And I am organising an expedition,' said Kubera. 'If it is successful, it will bring renown to Mudalur.'

Visvakarman looked at the congestion of cloudbanks.

'I shall adapt myself to reality,' he said. 'I shall attempt to take on the hue of my environment. Perhaps I can write like Crabbe or Thomas Hardy.'

'I can go or stay, as wished,' said Satyamurti. 'Presence or absence can make no real difference. Elsewhere I shall be as unnecessary as I am here.'

Lakshmi scowled triumphantly at Nalini. 'Useful suggestions, indeed!' she hissed, in a more than audible whisper. 'This is what comes of trying to consult the Brains Trust.'

Satyamurti, who was nearest to her, coloured a little.

'I have proposal if one is required. There is tall tree close to road by gorge's edge. If cut down properly it may precipitate itself across chasm and be capable of use as temporary bridge. Any of us can risk crossing to secure help.'

Kalyanasundaram shook his head. 'Not me. Slithering along trees is not my *métier*. Particularly not with a drop like that underneath.'

'I don't see why we need be involved,' Kubera protested, the tone of his voice a little distasteful at the prospect of being victimised by a common danger. 'It is simply a matter of organisation. Volunteers can always be found if the reward is suitable.'

'I am willing to make attempt,' Satyamurti said scornfully. 'You may offer me reward. I shall have pleasure of throwing it in chasm.'

He looked anxiously at Nalini as he said it. She told herself not to be vain, that he couldn't be doing it merely in order to gain her approbation. But his expression followed her, searching her thoughts, flinching away from the consequences it explored. He was not expecting to improve his prospects; but he wanted at least to create an occasion for gratitude.

'Anyway,' her father was saying, 'the sun is going down and it's too late to build bridges. And Murugesan's daughter is to be married. Perhaps the bad news can wait until after the wedding.'

'Quite,' agreed Kalyanasundaram. 'That's when the trouble always starts.'

'It is time to partake of refreshments,' Sambasivan said, 'and to recuperate from the day's labours.' His guests, who had done nothing all day, looked suitably exhausted. 'My daughter will sing if that is the general wish. Her execution

132

is classical even though her voice does not match the standards of her musicianship.'

He turned to Ernest.

'This is perhaps an infliction as far as you are concerned. If you prefer something less exotic, we have records of Gigli, the great Italian tenor.'

'Well, I'm not much of a musician,' Ernest replied, uncomfortably. He rubbed a couple of discords in his face. 'But I'd rather listen to something that has been born here. Even if I don't understand it, it'll help me to find out what's missing in myself.'

The remark pleased Nalini and she smiled back. She wasn't particularly anxious to sing, but she expected to be preferred to gramophone records. And because she was conscious of her own deficiencies she responded to people who knew that they themselves were incomplete.

There was a delay of a few minutes while the village drummer and the tambura player were sent for. Their arrival made Nalini feel disconcertingly splendid. She had been accustomed to provide her own accompaniment, squeezing and extorting it from the harmonium, hearing her voice apart from herself, disowned by herself, as the teacher's criticisms, wheedling and despairing, forced it remorselessly through the prescribed convulsions. She was the centre of all eyes now, no longer the theme of their demanding disapproval. She could control the music which had once commanded her. There was an audience to respond to her singing instead of a wall of whitewashed brick, lined with the portraits of more proficient ancestors. There were musicians beside her to enrich what she created. It was exhilarating but also a little intimidating. She found herself enjoying the shock of the combination.

The drummer began, a soft, dull, slow, infinitely varied tattoo, with each beat of the pattern set apart in its loneliness, the loneliness of raindrops, endlessly falling upon the drum of the night. Then the sounds of the plucked strings drew across the drumming, a vibrant monotony of something trembling and living over the deep, driving heartbeat of the silence. In front of the invocation of sound, her own voice floated and cascaded. She kept herself away from it, singing the song only with her lips, not allowing it to draw in her being. She had been the victim of this music before. Yet as she sang it now, its rigorous discipline seemed to give her strength and she found herself liberated in its severe and subtle formality. The force of order in the music unlocked an energy of order in herself, and without abandonment, with no sense of surrender she lost herself to the song until she could no longer hear her own voice sing it, until she was simply the truth which it relived.

She sang of the majesty of the divine, of the force of creation surging in the thunder, of the dance of change in its pure, timeless energy. The sun had gone down and she made the theme live against the velvet stealth of the darkness so that the words stood unchangeably in the foreboding hills. Her voice was clear and bright, refined in its precision, scholarly rather than passionate. She hadn't the honeyed throatiness which one expected from a good classical singer, and her parents, not finding it, had shaken their heads in reproof and told her that she would never be a musician. Yet now it appeared that her voice belonged to the music. The delicacy as well as the power of creation seemed to find expression in the restrained, fastidious singing, so ardent when one recognised its terms, like the girl herself sitting there, composed and tranquil, her hair rich with the perfume of all darknesses and her brown eyes drawing one into infinite depths.

She sang to nobody, she sang the song alone, neither aware of herself nor of an audience, though these were the vanities with which she had first begun. Yet the song was a question and an offering to each man, and each one felt that the garland was for him only. When she had finished the applause was much more than polite and she herself acknowledged it with more than politeness, with an inward blooming of dignity. There was a radiance in her face which was beyond elation, an intent, quiet beauty which was the contentment of knowing that the disciplines which had possessed her, clenched around her life, were now only means for the discovery of herself.

Ernest had listened with his familiar fascinated hostility to the endless involuting pattern of the music, the unchanging, infinite variety of the dance, the serpent's head swallowing its tail for ever. It was an elaborate game, he had often told himself; one could not judge the performance unless one knew the rules, and the rules themselves required a lifetime to master. It corresponded to nothing in the blood, an inexhaustible, sterile virtuosity handed on in the temples for ever, from teacher to student, a juggling act that had gone on unceasingly for four thousand years. He was angry at the sound of it, the cleverness of philosophy, the evasions of the vast myths, the supine submission, the passion for acceptance, a world of demons but without a devil, a world of change without the pulse of progress. How could she sit in that composure of loveliness, singing in that cool, faintly European voice, content in that discipline which was the musical echo of the other disciplines on which she must be broken? She sat serenely as if poised on a lotus, a lotus ordained to float away into the dark whirlpools of destruction and rebirth, the endless renewal that glistened in her singing. She was happy and hypnotised in the face of the juggernaut. If only he could shake her, plant the fury in her, beautify her with that essential discontent which was the pre-requisite of the will of progress. Why were no clouds reflected in her dark eyes? Had she read the stories of the slaying of Ravana only to forget the actual devils of hunger, disease and want that flourished outside in the dirt and need of her village? He was fascinated by her because she was so maddeningly intact. He wanted to crush her, reform her with reality.

Some of his feelings must have escaped into his face, for he heard Nalini reproving him with her apology.

'You must have found this extremely tiresome, Mr Jones.'

She said it with a slight, deliberate refinement to remind him that English was a foreign language to her. Her tone made him feel a little foreign himself.

'I like music that gets somewhere,' he replied.

'Progress!' boomed Sambasivan. 'It's a familiar Western heresy.'

Ernest's jaw moved forward. His face set in an expression of contemptuous and anguished pity. He began to look like a batsman arguing with an umpire.

'Nobody can stay where he is,' he proclaimed severely.

'Of course not,' said Sambasivan. 'It's better to march forward, demolishing all bridges. Just keep on going, even if you don't know where. Modern materialism has turned into a Pandora's box.'

He was pleased by his *non sequitur* and looked around him for a saying that would clinch it.

'Physician, heal thyself,' he ended triumphantly.

'There's nothing wrong with me,' said Ernest, stubbornly literal. 'Every man that's sent out here goes through a thorough check-up.'

'That's just it,' Sambasivan chortled. He was partly serious and partly flushed with the pleasure of scoring debating points. 'You're inoculated against tolerance too, I notice. Against understanding how others want to live.'

Nalini tried to smooth over the situation.

'Don't you think our guest might relish a game of billiards?'

Her father reacted encouragingly to the hint, propelling Ernest into the fifth circle.

'Billiards,' he explained, 'is played differently in Mudalur. It is a question of adaptation to the standard of living. Having considered the problem, my solution was as follows.'

He surveyed his captive audience as if he had just snookered it.

'Essentially the question is one of bounce. I asked myself why the bounce should be on the cushion. Why should it not be on the ball instead? This makes possible the use of tennis balls on a plain wooden table. Hence billiards is transformed into tenniards.'

He produced a tennis-racket with a four-foot handle, and screwed the top off, revealing the tip of a billiard-cue.

'India nowadays,' he proclaimed, 'is commendably full of multi-purpose projects. The merit of this particular invention is that a supply of chalk is hidden just below the racket face, thus making the cue automatically self-chalking. Moreover, the length gives one an advantage in volleying and service. Finally by attaching a piece of wood to the other end of the instrument, it is also possible to use it as a golf club.'

He ignored the expression of dismay on Ernest's face.

'Great inventions,' he continued, 'often have unexpected origins. The source for this was a Sears Roebuck catalogue. A combination of a jigger and corkscrew.'

He patted the new arrival understandingly on the shoulder.

'I see you are unappreciative, my dear friend. You object to liquor because of your Calvinist upbringing.'

'I'm not a Calvinist,' Ernest spluttered angrily.

'My mistake, my dear fellow. Your face made me think that you were chosen for something.'

Ernest looked at Nalini since there was nothing else sensible at which he could look. She was neither amused nor angry. He found himself first reassured and then annoyed by her composure. She was chameleon-like, he thought, in the manner of everything else in India, blending with the landscape in order to avoid destruction. She was one person abroad, another in this weird house, and in marriage she would become a third order of acceptance. Everything that

she could be had been decided in advance, a collection of snap-
shots in anyone's family album, the book closed when only
the preface had been written. And yet she remained herself,
a dark-haired girl, with a grace that came of walking on
many lotuses, a little pert, a little vain, and in the depths of
her Indian calm a trifle impish. What could he do to warn
her of the approaching accident? How was he to fill her
eyes with panic? What sense of calamity must he create to
preserve her?

He breathed a sigh, which he hoped was not one of resignation, picked up his tennis-racket, unscrewed the automatically self-chalking tip and swung it ferociously against
an ivory-coloured tennis ball.

II

The wedding took place as arranged by the parents, as
decreed by the stars, as wanted and then feared by the bridegroom and the bride. The sweet acrid smoke drifted into
everyone's faces so that what they could not see no longer
hurt them. Everyone ate too much and felt important.
Lakshmi cried copiously, first at the thought that the same
thing would happen to Nalini and then because of the fear
that this might not come to pass. The bride's parents thought
her wonderfully warm-hearted and the bride and bridegroom
touched her feet deferentially, making her feel like a public
institution. Sambasivan sat beside her with an unreal dignity
like a bank upon Bank Holiday, trying to counterpoise his
wife's impulsiveness by a remote decorum.

The bride and bridegroom looked hunted and contented, startled into seeing themselves, a frightened alliance built upon teak planks, in the spirals of smoke and the rings of the priests' invocation. The twigs, soaked in clarified butter, sizzled and snapped and the lonely selves came together in a composure of holiness. In the halves of a coconut the world broke open. They were the cynosure of all eyes, the proof of the normal, the reassurance that the fire would burn always, and stricken yet confident they took the seven steps, invoking the blaze into responsibility, the inner flame leaping as the outer subsided. When it was over, the groom put on the laborious insouciance of one who had experienced everything in his last birth. A photoflood was switched on and the cap flourished in front of the dusty lens. He stood his ground, confronting the camera as if it were a criminal, convincing himself that all things had been exposed. The bride was weighed down and trussed up, the damp red silk clinging to her oiled body, bedecked, replete with earrings and with warnings, sharp-nosed, already faintly vixen-faced, her eyes congealed with *mye*, staring fixedly over the wilted garlands. They were comic enough to remind everyone that they had only just ceased to be children, and serious enough to merit the blessings which their elders bestowed because it made them feel important. Affection was hung on them like the tired flowers they wore; they were the reason for an event that lived without them, forgetting them, snowing them under with exhortations, rancid jokes, moving on to the next marriage, the last illness, the child kicking softly, tugging infinity down, star-gazing into its intense sky of devotion.

The distinguished visitors to Mudalur stamped into the *pandal* out of the rain, nibbled at sweets and saw their own reflections. Kubera was critical of the ceremonies, which departed grievously from the classic model. The deviation, he prophesied with melancholy relish, would either doom the couple to sterility or to the production of an endless line of daughters. He offered them a second-class talisman and suggested that they co-operate in his scheme to commercialise the growing of Mudalur's mangoes. Kalyan saw the bride and bridegroom imprisoned and chained to tradition, as a pair of bookmarks in his monumental volume, and contemplated with pitying judiciousness the débris of their personalities, disinterred from under the avalanche of the dowry. He was delighted that so much had been spent on the marriage; it showed that no one was too poor for perversity and that even in ground where nothing seemed to grow there were still imbecilities that required to be rooted out.

Ernest had not been to a wedding previously. He was impressed by the total mobilisation which it achieved. Counting the five guests, the maximum possible number of three hundred and four were present. An exceptional opportunity had been missed, he reflected. If the BCG team had been there it could have dealt in one stroke with all positive reactors. Some of his colleagues, he recalled, were in favour of cinema shows, the entrance fee being an inoculation. But weddings were a more effective magnet: unlike movies they were capable of attracting even the blind and the deaf.

He looked at Nalini, trying to see her as the bride, gazing into an abandoned future, overwhelmed by roses of responsibility, transfixed and stupefied in the archetypal snapshot. She didn't belong in the picture he had arranged for her, or rather when she was in it the picture seemed to change. She was composed and animated, quietly firm and vivid in her modesty just as she had been coming out of the subway laden with books or by the lakeside with the orange flame of her sari curving against and lighting the heavy hues of the evergreens.

She saw the thought in his eyes and walked up to them.

'A wedding makes you think, doesn't it, Ernest?'

'It makes me think of the one that ought to take place.'

'Oh come,' she said. 'You can't be serious about that.'

'Why not? You can be happy in America. You can bring up children who mix the best of the two of us. You won't be shoved or squashed or decontrolled or be made into anything that you aren't.'

'Oh, Ernest,' she said. 'It's a wonderful description. It sounds exactly like a subway at rush hour.'

'Now it's you who aren't being serious.'

'I'll never forget my three years abroad,' she said, 'but I grew up in this place. It's queer and crummy and maddening. When I'm in it I'm often furious with it. When I leave it then something drops out of my heart. I can't forget the smell of its earth and the taste of its water and the craziness of the house in which I've lived and Father's pomposity and the way Mother watches over me like a dragon. I simply can't stand it and I've always belonged to it. The mangoes here taste different from anywhere else.'

He nodded his head. 'I guess I ought to understand that. I feel the same way about the flea-bitten, one-street burg in which I grew up. But I feel worried about you, worried about the way in which you're drifting like a sleepwalker into this arranged marriage business. How can you be happy with someone you don't even know?'

'Oh, it isn't as arbitrary as all that,' she said. 'You're not expected to put up with anyone you really detest. And your parents have your interests at heart: they're not ones to make irresponsible choices. After that it's just a question of what two average people can make of each other, given goodwill and a sense of mutual respect. It usually works out. It ought to, if you believe in people. Now don't you find that explanation completely convincing?'

'Definitely not,' said Ernest. 'It doesn't sound like the truth, it sounds like a Ph.D. dissertation. And now that you've wrapped up your wedding-day philosophy, will you please tell me which of those second-class bums is destined to be your soul-mate of the average?'

'I don't have to marry any of them.'

'I thought so,' said Ernest. 'But one day your mother will tell you to be serious.'

'She thinks they're all beneath consideration.'

'One day she'll find the answer you can't detest.'

Nalini pursed her lips a little. 'In that case, I'll marry him,' she decided. 'If he's tall, slim, handsome, exciting and intelligent and really adores me, what have I to grumble about? But that's in the future. Let's talk about *this* wedding now. Don't you think it's a gorgeous show for such a small place?'

'It's a waste of money in a country that can't afford it.'

'And what do you suppose we *can* afford?' Her tone became mildly sarcastic. 'Plumbing, tube-wells and a lower death-rate, perhaps.'

'You can afford to try,' he told her, sententiously.

Her face crimsoned. 'Really, Ernest, you should live with us a little more before you start to lecture us. Go out into the fields and watch our people work. Try to plough behind bullocks that are dropping from starvation. See what you can grow on land that's been exhausted.'

'I'd put nitrogen into it.'

'And pay for it with what?'

'With some of the stuff you throw away at weddings.'

'It's easy to find answers like that,' she said. 'To have a prefabricated remedy for everything: slaughter our surplus cows, exterminate our monkeys, keep the population within reasonable limits and finance everything with the wealth of the Maharajahs. It's logical and in the end it's probably right; but you mustn't let it drain away too much of the colour that makes our lives worth living.'

'I'm sorry,' he said. 'I guess it's the way I've been trained. I like to push things in the direction of tidiness. But of course, it's for you to choose what you want.'

'And you don't think we want weddings?'

'How can you choose when you can't even choose your husband?'

He could see from her expression that his words had gone home, but he was prudent enough not to go further. There was an uncertain silence while she fidgeted with her right foot. She was going to ask about his work when Raman came up.

'Disgusting waste, this wedding.'

'Couldn't agree more,' said Ernest.

Raman glared at him. 'You're a foreigner and your agreement is of no consequence.'

'We've got to agree,' Ernest proclaimed with determined cordiality. 'If we understand each other we can't help agreeing.'

He mounted his platform of principles expectantly, trying to clasp Raman's hand in a moral handshake.

'Agreement,' the other man snorted. 'I know your sort, you never give something for nothing. The more you offer, the more dangerous you are.'

'Now see here,' Ernest protested, alerting his jaw. 'We've got to go into this on a basis of partnership. We're buddies together in the war against want.'

He thumped Raman's back to pound home the fraternity.

'It's really a crusade and not a war. A *jehad* fought with D.D.T., not dynamite.'

'You want to poison us with it.'

'Poison you? Nonsense. It wouldn't hurt a fly.'

'Then how is it supposed to kill mosquitoes?'

'I was speaking figuratively,' Ernest explained.

'In other words you were lying. One lie leads back to another. I know the face of hypocrisy when I see it.'

'You know darned well that the stuff wipes out malaria.'

'Then why are you letting us have it?'

'For your own good, of course.'

'You can't sell it, so you want to dump it on us.'

'We're only doing something you can't yet do, for nothing.'

'And you'll never let us do it,' Raman raged. 'You want

145

us to depend on this dope. Every time a mosquito bites us
you want us to come to you moaning for help. If you must
give us something give us a factory with which to make the
stuff. Then we'll be free of you for ever. We can stand on
our own feet. We don't have to go down on our knees
before you.'

Ernest tried again.

'Certainly you've got to stand on your own feet. Self-help
is the basis of any foreign aid programme. Anything else is
dangerous for the patient.'

'So now we're in hospital,' Raman exploded. 'It's you
who are sick. Just look at your foreign policy.'

Ernest denied himself an agonising reappraisal.

'I'm not a politician,' he said patiently persistent. 'Our
job is to get to a good neighbourliness beyond politics.
You've got to lift yourself up by your bootstraps and all we're
doing is to try to give you the boots. Then it's up to you to
make your initiatives airborne.'

'We're a barefoot people,' Raman said. 'We became free
without anybody helping us. We can build our future without other people's charity.'

He said it with a kind of derelict dignity that was an
improvement on his earlier indignation. It impressed Ernest
enough to restrain him from retorting. As for Nalini, while
disapproving of most of what Raman said, she had listened
to him with fascinated exasperation. There was something
mesmeric about his personality that made one reach instinctively for the rolling-pin. He could only be intense when he
was being didactic. He lived completely in his pose. Even if
he were to wash his face, he would do so with the air of a

man ridding his country of a pernicious influence. Yet like many saviours he was probably something of a hypocrite. His disregard for dress was a trifle too studied, his hair too photogenically disarranged. His teeth, which flashed attractively in a firm yet mobile mouth, were almost certainly made white by imported toothpaste. He had nice shoulders, sleek but strong, and smouldering eyes which she would have liked to see laugh. In fact he was quite good-looking with a faintly refined and therefore irritating surliness. His voice was unexpectedly vibrant for a person only two inches taller than herself. It was an agitator's voice undoubtedly, but, saying the right things, it could be so much more golden. What a pity that such assets should be wasted, she thought, but people like Raman had a place in life – one felt obliged to pummel them into something better and in the excitement of improvement one seemed to discover a little of one's own self.

These reflections in her eyes made them look mischievous so that both Ernest and Raman were puzzled by what they saw. She was frivolous like her class, Raman concluded; spoilt by her father's modest wealth, corrupted further by a foreign education, condemned in marriage to some anglicised imbecile with a position in the government, what could she do but move with desperate inconsequence through her bright world of rickety inanities? Yet if she were compelled into significance, if she scrubbed floors, steamed lentils and drew buckets of water from a deep enough well, she could be brought back to a modest and peasant dignity. It would be a difficult process though, considering how comprehensively she had already been ruined, and in India there were more important mistakes which demanded correction more urgently and emphatically.

Having dismissed her from his mind, he turned his back on her. He had to suppress a slight feeling of disappointment when she failed to reprove him for being rude. She in her turn thought him disgustingly bad-mannered, but she told herself that it was not worth while to say so, when there were more fundamental reasons for detesting him.

Ernest waited till he was out of earshot. 'Didn't make much of an impression on him,' he said.

'Don't mind the discouragements,' Nalini smiled. 'You're doing a wonderful piece of work.'

His face brightened. 'D'you really think so?'

'Of course,' she said confidently. 'A better chance to live, an ever so slightly better world to live in. It's worth a little snubbing to achieve that.'

He shook his head regretfully, but not at her remarks.

'You're so out of place here – a girl like you, vital and generous. You ought to be doing something constructive, something important, helping your country to move into its future or at least living your own life and really finding yourself. Instead of which, you're stagnating in this backwater, waiting to be married.'

'But Dr Jones,' she teased him, 'you've destroyed the only way out.'

'Oh, no, I haven't,' he said. 'I've built the bridge back to reality. Marry me and I'll take you away from all this. We can bounce all over Asia in my jeep. We'll be married in Park Avenue with choirboys singing and champagne for everyone at the Commodore afterwards and you in one of those fabulous Fifty-seventh Street outfits that only make sense because one's wife is in them. And from then onwards everything will be different. Marry me and make it all come true. The two of us can reform the world together.'

'But, Ernest,' she said, 'do you really think one ought to be married in church?'

'Where else do you suppose a respectable girl can get married?'

'It's so much more sensible just to sign the register. Think of the money we'd save. We could make the down payment on a Cape Cod house in Larchmont.'

'Well, I've never heard anything so ridiculous. A civil wedding! It's mean and soulless and sordid! How can a marriage stay right unless it starts right? I want a beginning I can always remember. I want you to say "I do" in a train with six yards of tulle, white and incredible as the powder snow on the hills. I want it said to me with stars in your eyes and not with a ball-point pen clutched in your right fist.'

'If you really feel as strongly as that,' she said, 'why do you disapprove of the wedding that we're having now?'

He grinned shamefacedly. 'I guess I can afford it and India can't.'

'You know that's nonsense,' she said. 'The poor need poetry even more than we do. A wedding is like a rainbow to them, reaching up and over many hills of drabness. If you don't believe in the existence of rainbows, how can you fight for the crock of gold at the end? So stop being dishonest and enjoy yourself. Atone for your Puritanism by eating six *jilabis*.'

She took his hand gently, smiled into his eyes and led him unprotesting into the mêlée.

III

When the talk was extinguished and the fire burned out and the bright paper of the lanterns crumpled, the emptiness came down as it always did. The remembrance of new clothes was put away. The flash of bangles, the scent of hope and laughter, the humble gaudiness, were set aside and supplanted by the monotony, as the rain splashed softly or drummed into the thatches and as the river flowed evenly into the endless night.

Murugesan sat in his hut beside the table. Without Padma's voice opening memories and joining them to promises, the walls of the small room seemed to have drawn closer, so that the room itself was like an enormous safe, enclosing the black steel box and Mudalur's treasure. The box had the words 'Property of Hillview Estates' fastened to the top in nickel-plated letters. He polished them with the soft chamois as he did every evening, and then applied Brasso to the combination lock.

It was a fine strong box, worthy of a fine table, and the table was indeed so fine and splendid that it occupied approximately six-tenths of the room. But nothing except the steel box was ever allowed on top of it. When his wife Savithri insisted upon sewing she did so out of doors or in the kitchen and even the small bronze Ganapati which she almost submerged in miniature garlands had to sit in the corner, on top of a packing-case, where it looked reproach-fully at the black steel box towering over it like some superior deity. The family ate on the floor as they had always done before the box arrived, with Murugesan and Savithri just outside the table legs and the children crammed underneath, until Padma's head began to hit the top, by which time her parents deduced that it was time to have her married. When they slept, it was in more or less the same way on the same floor, except when it was fine enough to sleep outside. Then Murugesan would lie alone in the hut, on the bench next to the table, his fingers clutching the handle of the box so that any would-be thief could approach the combination only over his body.

He polished the brass lock insistently, passionately, till it glittered and shone like gold under the unsteady light of the kerosene lamp. Then he adjusted the combination, listening secretively to the sound of the tumblers as they clicked into place. Gently he opened the lid. His wedding photograph lay on top and underneath it, his frequently thumbed defence of deficit financing. It was only then that one came to the crisp stacks of notes which he refused to touch except with newly washed hands, and the coins fresh from the mint, piled neatly in their separate compartments. He took one of the wads out and held the money to the light, perusing the watermarks with a practised eye. A faint expression of dis-taste crossed his face. They were all identical and there were millions of others like them. They lacked the uniqueness which was the signature of the true artist.

His own talent had matured early and even as a child he drew with a delicate beauty of line that marked him out for achievements in the fine arts. His family could not afford to send him to school and when he was only twelve years old they told him that it was time for him to earn the fragments of a living. He found himself a job in a wayside *pan* shop, on the outskirts of a small town remote from his village. The shop also sold aerated waters and this enabled him to put his gift for design to practical use. He produced labels of ravishing beauty and exotic promise such as Pomegranate Squash, Guava Essence, Nilgiri Pear Extract, Elephant Brand, Peacock Brand and finally Imperial and Ahimsa Brand so that his ware maintained a judicious political balance. All the bottles were filled with the same bittersweet, sticky, aerated, worthless liquid, but the colours varied like the clothes of his clients and when the marble in the neck of the bottle was banged in, the stuff squirted all over the purchaser's face, which proved the potency of the aeration and evidently gave the customer what he wanted. From the three hundred per cent profits of this enterprise Murugesan was able to buy a *jutka*, in the rear of which he sat regally blowing a conch, while a two-piece orchestra played in the interior. His task was to dispense mouth-watering accounts of forthcoming film masterpieces to sad-eyed citizens who could never afford a ticket. The owner of the movie house went bankrupt in due course; but Murugesan's capital and popularity increased. He disliked towns though, even if they were only small towns. He was afraid of the feeling of anonymity which diluted and drained away the strength of the artist. His heart hankered after the compact truth of his village which he could possess all at once and within which he could play a creative part.

In producing his cinema posters he had acquired equipment which could be used in various ways. These ways began to form in his mind more clearly. He bought newspapers and, when he read them backwards as better men than he did, he found on the last but one page discouraging accounts of financial crises and of the Government's need for more money. A man to whom he had once sold raspberry sherbet had told Murugesan frequently that the individual citizen should take part in the process of government. This man was now a prominent politician, which convinced Murugesan that his wisdom was profound. Murugesan decided to put two and two together and to add up the total in his village.

When he came home he told the villagers that the banknotes they had were of inferior quality and should be replaced immediately by his own product. Some misgivings were expressed at first; but the people were impressed by the equipment which Murugesan installed and by the undoubted skill with which he used it. When the first notes were produced there was no question that they were æsthetically superior to the imported product, besides being printed on paper that was twice as thick and durable. Those who used them found that they were as effective as any other banknote. The village was self-sufficient and herein lay the source of Murugesan's strength. He was a passionate advocate of rural self-sufficiency. The village produced its own *khadi*, he argued – that it should do so was part of the country's basic philosophy. Why should it not produce its own currency also, thereby relieving the Government of an unnecessary burden?

The deep simplicity of Murugesan's thought convinced the villagers of his intellectual greatness. In normal circumstances they would have honoured him as a man of genius by listening to him reverentially, putting garlands round his neck and paying no attention whatever to his teachings. But the circumstances were not normal and the fact was that Murugesan's programme, quite apart from its philosophical merits, was clearly bringing prosperity to the village. More was produced. New jobs became available. People worked harder and found they could eat better. Thus Murugesan succeeded in creating the state of confidence that was the pre-requisite of currency reform.

He was surprised at his own success. Since he was an artist and not an entrepreneur his methods were simple and almost saintly. He dispensed notes when the need for them was proven and he kept for himself only the austere minimum that he wanted. He made no fortune and no one around him did, but he became the custodian of a state of security and happiness.

Because of his scrupulously high standards, his restraint in manufacture, and the comparative isolation of his village, it was over a year before the law became aware of him. When the officers arrived he himself conducted them proudly around the village, pointing out the new school and the improvements to the temple. Then he showed them the press. The production runs, he explained, were extremely short and the design was varied subtly with each batch so that forgery of his notes was out of the question. Naturally such refinements were impossible in mass production by the Government, but in cottage industries the craftsman had his chance.

He was bewildered when they unceremoniously hand-cuffed him, destroyed his equipment and confiscated his currency. Although his activities had been conducted with full public knowledge and co-operation he was denounced vehemently as a liar and a cheat. Bail was set at a preposterously high figure; even so his people were willing to pay it but could only do so in the currency which he himself had manufactured and which the Government high-handedly refused to accept.

Murugesan's fortunes were now abruptly reversed. The notes he had printed so carefully and lovingly were declared to be totally valueless. Those who still hoped to make use of them were threatened with the grimmest resources of the law. Consequently all those who had accepted Murugesan's notes (and that included virtually every inhabitant) found themselves suddenly penniless and fell into bondage to neighbouring money-lenders. Production collapsed. Unemployment grew. The village sank into starvation and misery. Angry voices were raised against Murugesan, accusing him of treason and demanding his head.

In jail Murugesan read as much he he could and prepared himself to conduct his own defence. The courtroom was filled with those whom he had ruined and who now demanded that he be ruined also. The prosecution condemned him in ringing tones as a forger, a fraud and an enemy of society. Murugesan made his answer with dignity. He had amassed no money and his hands were clean. From his aerated water days he had always given the people what they wanted and this, as the court well knew, was a basic tenet of democratic society. The soundness of his theories was proved by the prosperity they had brought to his village until the catastrophic intervention of certain misguided officials who had obviously never read Lord Keynes.

As for the monstrous accusation of forgery, he could not but treat it with the contempt that it deserved. He, Murugesan, was an artist and an individualist incapable of forging anything so promiscuous and common as a Government currency note. His notes were designed by himself, and signed by himself instead of by the Auditor-General. Nobody in his senses could mistake them for Government currency and if people had preferred them it was because they were different and better. A kind of peaceful competition had taken place and the customer, who was always right, had chosen the superior product.

His points were well taken, but there was no one to take them. His hostile audience seemed to include no economists and the judge, who was no philosopher, gave him five years.

When he emerged his country was independent. He had been in the right jail and had come to know the right people so that it was with hope that he called on the prison colleague who had shared his cell with him and was now an eminent bureaucrat. He presented his card to the *chaprass* with a fraternal flourish: A. R. Murugesan, Design Consultant. The *chaprass* looked at the name with inborn suspicion, tempered a little by the gilt on the card. He disappeared into the house. Five minutes later he rushed out, his face convulsed with contempt. Murugesan was ejected in a torrent of invective. The shoe drummed a tattoo of rejection on his back. The other addresses were different, but the shoe felt the same. Murugesan received the affronts with dignity. He limped along queerly erect since he was unable to stoop, now that his spine had been thoroughly bastinadoed. In the market-place he stopped outside a resplendent American car. He had eaten nothing all day and was dizzy. The chromium bumpers glittered like his country's budget. The front seat was three times as large as his cell. A sausage-shaped dog sat in a corner of it, vigorously chewing a treatise on public finance. Murugesan recoiled and a surge of perfume swept over him. He opened the door to divert the inundation. It congealed into a woman. She had gimlet eyes, a skin like yesterday's yoghurt and was dressed expensively to resemble a sofa.

'My, my,' she cooed. 'You're the best dressed beggar I've seen.'

'I ask for nothing,' Murugesan said with dignity.

'You don't even whine,' she squealed back. 'You haven't yet swallowed your pride. What a relief from all these spineless cripples.'

She threw a banknote at him negligently. An eddy of wind seized it and swept it under the car. He reached for it and as he did so the engine snarled into life and the wheels spun forward. He got his hand back in time to avoid it being crushed, but the side of the car caught him and almost flung him against the pavement. He regained his balance and, bewildered by the collision, salaamed instinctively and amazedly. The car screeched off and he could hear the woman's voice shrilling over the dog's bark.

'Insufferable,' she was screaming. 'You're generous to the swine and they can't even get out of the way.'

He held on to the banknote with mixed feelings. It was a

mass-produced commodity, an inherent negation of crafts-manship, but it bought him a meal, unlike the superior product. With the change he had left he was able to persuade the refugee who sat next to him to sell him a partnership in a soft drink stall. It was strategically located outside a cosmetic shop. Rich women emerged from it with reassuring regularity accompanied by thirsty and raucous brats. The number of foreigners had increased steadily since independence came and the foreigner left. Murugesan appealed to them with his air of abstraction and the aristocratic stiffness induced by numerous hidings. He was almost always able to sell more than he expected. Yet though the turnover was substantial and the profits exorbitant he could not help feeling the lack of an inner vitality. He was appalled by the new generation of customers. They were hurried and harried and possessed by aimlessness. Whenever he saw them, they were pressing forward, intense, purposive and dedicated to heaven knows what since they themselves had not the faintest idea of it. Sometimes it seemed to Murugesan that they were more anxious to implement the five-year plan than to have it discussed. He found himself grieved at this devotion to action at the expense of understanding. Though his income rose his spirits steadily sank. The days passed, the implacable shadows lengthened and he read the newspapers more and more desperately backwards, seeking the advertisement that was to change his life. He found it eventually, under an offer of surplus brassières. There was no question that it was the right inquiry. Reading it, he had a deep and exalting sense of recognition, of having met the author in a previous birth.

158

'Wanted. Keeper of Cash for Unprecedented Enterprise. Ph.D. less important than Creative Imagination
and Talent for the Unorthodox.'

He snipped it out of the page, underlined the words with
Subtle Surrender lipstick and wrapped the cutting solicitously in a wad of banknotes. Then he sold his partnership
at a two thousand three hundred per cent profit and, carrying
only a tin of Ecstasy Essence, he headed hotfoot for the
heavenly hills. From Arkayam station he pressed on like a
man possessed, overtaking no less than one hundred and
eighteen other candidates. Many had abandoned hope in the
forest, convinced that the author of the advertisement did
not exist and that only mockery lay beyond the green and
ghoulish darkness. Others were already on their way down,
gibbering aimlessly and eating bananas and jackfruit.
Murugesan swept past them with the deceptive leisureliness
of a long-distance runner husbanding his strength for the
last lap. A few applicants pitied him; several admired him;
the majority pursued him, having convinced themselves that
a man so obsessed could not be entirely mistaken. They toiled
hysterically up the coils of the road until the stranglehold of
the forest released them, fifty-six exhausted men completing
the long march in various stages of dysentery and disgust.

When the survivors had gathered their wits and were
questioned they professed various altruistic motives for their
coming. The majority wanted the job to marry their
daughters; a substantial number needed it to send their sons
to college; and some confessed that they had answered the
advertisement chiefly to keep their mothers-in-law from nag-

ging. Only a very few were prepared to admit that they sought the position in order to fill their own bellies. When Murugesan's turn came his answer was simple and authoritative. He wanted the job, he said, because of his passion for money. Lakshmi hooted with derision when she heard this, but Sambasivan recognised the profound sense of vocation that lay buried in the remark. He engaged Murugesan on the spot. The jail sentence did not deter him. The family cook, he recalled, was a pacifist gone berserk who had spent eight years in prison for slicing off his wife's ears. Lakshmi had howled with anguish when he was hired, but he had settled down to serve delectable dinners with no evidence in them of either noses or navels. Instead, his homicidal drives had been sublimated in pounding and grinding *iddalis* of succulent smoothness. The situation was the same now, he argued. One needed insight to evaluate the facts, but to anyone possessing the gift of psychological penetration it was plain that one who despised the official currency as much as Murugesan did was extremely unlikely ever to abscond with it.

Murugesan did not abscond. He guarded the steel box and its contents with a resigned solicitude for the misguided halfwits who desired no better alternative. He made his peace in Mudalur. The lengthening shadows deepened and soothed his thoughts; they were no longer knives made out of the darkness, moving towards a wall, encircling a stake. There was an ordinary, unspectacular serenity in this place which seemed to lie naturally on the edge of everything. In the begging bowl of the hills one's questions lay down to rest even when they were not answered by the stars. He buried his memories, watched the clouds march past and waited for the first rains of each summer to splash upon his tongue like aerated water.

Now he sat in his hut looking at the face of the man opposite, two feet away from him, questioning and uneasy in the slurring shadows of the kerosene lamp. He studied him gravely and dispassionately as if he were proposing to engrave him on a coin.

'The wedding's over,' Murugesan said.

The other man coughed. 'You recall, there are certain formalities.'

Murugesan reached up to the table. He had opened the steel box earlier when there was no one in the house, for the combination was secret and not even the click of the tumblers was allowed to suggest it. He took down the cloth bundle and undid the knot with magisterial solemnity as if rectifying a confusion in his guest's nature. There was a thin wad of banknotes in it and two muslin bags in which the coins clinked as he laid them on the floor.

'You may verify the dowry if you wish.'

'Counting is unnecessary,' the other man said. His tones suggested that there were deeper doubts.

'That is well,' said Murugesan. 'The best of all banknotes is confidence.'

Padma's father-in-law swallowed hard. He looked anxiously and mutely at Murugesan, his eyes and the tattoo of his fingers outlining the question which it was indecent to ask. Murugesan returned his stare impassively. It was not proper, he suggested, to ask such questions even with one's eyes. Then as the other man wilted, Murugesan's mouth turned down, setting his face in that familiar expression of reproving resignation and fastidious distaste.

'It is the inferior thing,' he said aloofly.

The other man's face brightened with relief. He restrained himself from precipitately grabbing the money. Leaning forward, he looked into the treasurer's eyes with what he apparently hoped was understanding.

'Frustration,' he said consolingly, 'is the lot of the true artist.'

4

The Expedition

I

THE NEXT DAY was also a morning of great events. The wedding was over and the divorce from civilisation now had to be patched up. The route back to Arkayam and to the queries of Mobile H.Q. was to be made whole again by a few well-judged strokes of the axe from Kesavan, that great joiner, dovetailer of hopes and expert healer of schisms, who now sat in the sun of Mudalur's forthcoming adulation, the genuine sunlight being as usual absent. He girded his loins and inspected his weapons, imbibed various potations to elevate his spirits and called thunderously upon his adoring wife to anoint his heroic muscles with jasmine oil. From the lubrications and the libations he arose a new man, or at least a man more polished, uncertain of himself but certain what he was meant for. Erratically he advanced upon his fate, capering down through the puddles of the road with a spirited and yet delicate clumsiness. His heaven-given weapons were held aloft, thrice blessed by Kubera and the local priests, sharpened in the expectant sacrifice of the entire village's Tuesday production of butter. Everyone followed him since there was nothing else to do. Some doubted his qualities as a man of destiny, arguing that one who could not see straight would be unable to saw straight; but there was clearly no alternative since Kesavan owned the only saw in Mudalur. So he danced on unhindered through the chest-beating rain, brimming with booze and bursting with self-confidence, singing songs that were alternately obscene and warlike, until his razor-sharp, infallible, double-dealing vision focused on the green fuzz, the sacred tree of his destiny. With a cry of ardour he flung himself upon it and, bitten immediately by a horde of red ants, recoiled from it with a loud howl of pain. Then he circumnavigated the tree, nearly disappearing into the ravine while doing so, and, having completed his survey, prostrated himself in front of his objective. He must at this stage have been overwhelmed by humility since four men and a couple of well-directed kicks were needed to restore him to the vertical position. The strategic zone on the tree was ringed in yellow paint; and Kesavan, calling on the spirits of his ancestors and on the Minister for Agriculture, retired to a distance of twenty feet. Here he composed himself, rolled his eyeballs, flexed his muscles and passionately embraced the yellow sari of his wife until he was persuaded that the tree was elsewhere. Propelled in the correct direction, he whirled the axe terrifyingly round his head like a cross between a discus-thrower and a demented dervish and plunged it unexpectedly into the centre of the target. Intoxicated by his precision he struck again and at exactly the same spot. Murmurs of approbation rose from the gathering. His wife, who had no wish to be confused with a tree any longer, retired modestly behind a convenient bush. Leaping yet higher and whirling even more furiously, the axe of Kesavan crashed forward and struck again and yet again relentlessly, till weakened and willed down by the deadly strength of those lunges the top of that tall means of deliverance started to tremble. Then Kesavan was made to desist, though not without some peril to the life of the man who effected his disengagement from that cataclysmic war-dance. One end of the saw was placed in Kesavan's hands; the other was given to the village blacksmith who despised no one as much as the village carpenter. The two sawed frantically, venomously, in an electrifying, uprooting oscillation of hate. The trunk of the tree tottered. It lurched towards the chasm. Then it plunged downwards in an exultation of voices.

In normal circumstances the tree would have been long enough. But the circumstances in Mudalur were never normal. The rains had been the worst in living memory, which meant that it was even wetter than last year. It was certainly wet enough decisively to undermine the opposite bank. The weight of the tree's branches clutched at it and then sank through it, inexorably tearing the side of the ravine away. Then the tree plummeted down in a torrent of mud and débris. There was a horrified silence broken only by the whirring of a cine-camera.

Everyone turned to look fascinated at Ernest. He uncoupled his eye from the view-finder, shut off the motor with a click of satisfaction and put the equipment back in his gadget bag.

'It's a ninety-foot job now,' he said. 'An even more major engineering project.'

II

Apart from Lakshmi, who added her landslide of lamentations to the débris, no one in the gathering was greatly depressed. Most of the visitors were absorbed in their pet projects. Moreover, as Kalyan pointed out, time was in their favour; it was inconceivable that an American could be missing for long without a rescue operation of mammoth dimensions being organised. Even at this moment Super Fortresses were probably plunging through the thunderclouds, combing the wilderness in search of the missing hero. Kubera agreed enthusiastically: the full moon was only one night away; if corned beef were to cascade from heaven at the same time as the mangoes were brought down from the mountain-top, the miracle of Mudalur would need no further emphasis. And once the juggernaut of illusion had begun to move, prosperity would follow stupefied in its wake. A stainless steel bridge would be built over the ravine and a three-lane highway to Arkayam down it.

Meanwhile, the guests could continue to promenade in their respective circles like planets circling round the sun of Nalini. Time passed in a relaxing, reassuring monotony. The rain fell solidly, blotting out all memories, and when it was over everything seemed to be more and more itself. The catering was excellent; Lakshmi's performance seemed to improve steadily as her detestation of her visitors increased. Reality was a satisfyingly long way off, in a tumbledown railway station, on the other side of a regrettably impassable forest. The collection of freaks that seemed to inhabit Mudalur gave each new arrival a richly reassuring sense of his own sanity.

In short the situation was not at all unpleasant, and it was even more pleasant to be able to enjoy it while complaining piteously of the hardships it imposed. The population trudged up the hill with tragic faces and not too heavy hearts. Raman buzzed through the procession livid with triumph. Foreign intervention had revealed itself in its true colours. The jeep was the symbol of all evil and any half-wit could see that whatever it brought, it more than took away. Atom bombs would follow in the wake of insect powder. The isolation of the village was only the first step in its extermination. The people listened to him, gravely nodding their noses, but were unable to be too angry with the gadget-laden foreigner who seemed to exist only in order to fumigate. They recognised in him a kindred queerness.

Nalini walked back, admiring the colours of the forest, colours so dense that they sometimes seemed almost to suffocate its growth. She stopped in front of a bunch of flowers, blazing and limp with its own vividness. She moved forward to pick it. Her foot caught against an exposed root, and she fell. When she tried to pick herself up her face became twisted with pain.

'I'm afraid I've sprained it,' she said.

'In a place like this,' wailed Lakshmi. 'Miles away from home up this eighth-rate imitation of a mule-track. How are we ever going to get you back safely?'

'You don't have to worry,' Ernest said. 'I'd be happy to give her a lift.' He smiled a little condescendingly. There had been general amusement at his driving down in the jeep instead of walking to the ravine like everyone else. Now his eccentricity would serve a useful purpose.

Lakshmi sniffed dubiously at the offer. 'So far Nalini has only sprained her ankle. We wouldn't want her to dislocate her spine into the bargain.'

'I got four-wheel drive on this outfit,' Ernest protested.

Nalini threw up her hands. 'Please, please, I simply want to get home. If you object to my being jolted in a jeep I'm quite prepared to be sea-sick in a stretcher. I'm sure the four gallant men who were good enough to ask for my hand in marriage won't object to carrying it for a paltry six miles.'

The four stalwart suitors looked doubtfully at their biceps.

'Thank you for your consideration,' smiled Nalini. She held out her hand to Ernest, who assisted her into the jeep. It shot off in a cloud of dust and disappeared round the corner with the cavalcade plodding patiently behind. Ten minutes later they caught up with it. It was parked precariously on the kerb of the road which happened to be a two-and-a-half-foot boulder. Ernest had disappeared professionally under the chassis. Various expert clangings and thumpings were heard. Then Ernest's boots began to signal triumphantly.

'It's the magneto,' he announced, emerging. 'It shouldn't take long to fix that.'

Sambasivan looked doubtful. 'Are you quite sure it wouldn't be better to walk?'

'She simply can't walk. As a doctor, I absolutely forbid it. But you don't have to worry, I know every nut on this war-horse. I'll get her home exactly like I promise. As for the rest of you, you'd better start moving before it gets any later. And have a hot lunch ready for Nell because she'll need it.'

Sambasivan glanced at his guests. Visvakarman seemed about to compose an ode on Starvation. Kubera succeeded in looking both prosperous and piteous.

'Our duty is to look after them,' he said, turning to Lakshmi.

'And my daughter's fate is of no consequence whatever?'

'Hospitality must always come before the family.'

'I give my word she'll be O.K.,' Ernest said.

'Please go, Mother,' Nalini appealed heroically. 'How can I presume to weigh myself against the convenience and well-being of my suitors? Every *ladoo* of which this accident deprives them is going to sit like a cannon-ball on my conscience.'

There was a whispered and hectic consultation. Then the procession moved on with Lakshmi looking agonisedly back, gesticulating wordless warnings towards her daughter. Ernest buried himself in the interior of the engine and proceeded to make sounds as if he were shoeing a horse. After ten minutes' fiddling, he extricated himself again and removed a collection of centipedes from the sparking-plugs. He wriggled into the driver's seat. They were alone in the forest with the faint, persistent texture of its sounds laid like a film over the thick, pulsing silence. He looked hard at Nalini. There was a fire in his eyes which she hadn't previously seen there. His hands slipped off the wheel and instinctively she edged back. Then she realised with chagrin that he was only reaching for his cine-camera.

At that moment there was a crashing, trampling noise and an elephant emerged into the road behind them. He eyed the odd scene with interest. Mudalur's was a backward forest and the elephant had apparently not kept abreast of the latest developments in symbolic fiction. So instead of charging the jeep he proceeded to admire it. He was not a particularly large animal, but for Nalini he was more than large enough. She stood up, completely oblivious of her ankle and barely managing to stifle a scream. The elephant's attention was focused immediately on her sari's riot of colour. He looked at her with that appealing lewdness which movie monsters reserve for lovely ladies. What he saw must have stirred his higher instincts, for he trumpeted reassuringly and raised his trunk in a beneficient salutation.

While these courtesies were being exchanged there was plenty of time for the jeep to move off. But Nalini, listening frantically for the healthy roar of a six-cylinder engine, was unable to hear anything of the sort. Instead there came to her horrified ears the unmistakable chirp of a clockwork motor. When she whipped around her worst suspicions were realised. Ernest Hamilton Jones was standing bolt upright in the driver's seat, his eyes glued to the view-finder of the cine-camera.

This was too much for the elephant, which made for the jeep with gusto. Ernest saw the animal zooming at him through his zoom lens. He dropped his camera and picked up his untried and trusty .582, unconditionally guaranteed to stop three and a half tons of African elephant stone-cold at eighty-six inches. At sixty-eight yards he pulled the trigger and knocked himself into the windscreen with the recoil. The elephant, which was not African, kept on coming.

Fortunately for Nalini her reactions were not delayed by the events of her short life passing before her in review. All she could remember were those tales of Siberian sleigh-rides in which fleeing aristocrats dispensed the more edible members of their family to packs of pursuing and famished wolves. There was no spare relative in the back of the jeep; all she could find was a bunch of green bananas. She threw it out with the strength born of desperation; it was far more effective than any .582. The elephant braked hard in a flurry of mud and gravel and, trumpeting gaily, picked up the peace-offering and began to wolf it down. Obviously he preferred them young and tender. Time had been bought, but there was precious little of it and Nalini realised with terror that there were no bananas left.

'Start the car,' she screamed. 'Get her going, you cretinous numb-skull.'

She need not have been so unlady-like. Ernest Hamilton Jones had already extracted himself from the windscreen and had hurtled into action with a dash that was worthy of a racing motorist. The engine hummed happily; it was producing power instead of cooking caterpillars. The jeep shot off in a spectacular demonstration of the merits of four-wheel drive. Behind them, the elephant watched the performance of the strange animal perplexed, and decided not to waste time competing with its antics. He finished his bananas and chased a hog into a hole.

Ernest tore round a corner and twisted through a hairpin before easing his foot off the accelerator. He stopped to look at Nalini, who was still standing upright, gazing wanly into the steppes of Siberia.

'You are sure you're O.K.?' he asked her.

'Oh, I'm feeling simply wonderful,' Nalini said. Having made that gallant over-statement, she collapsed demurely to the floor-boards.

III

When she recovered consciousness she found herself in Arcady. The birds were singing, several of them outside her head. The air was crisp and lucid with a pleasant feeling of menthol about it. The rustle of the leaves and the purling of the brook were unimaginably unlike the sound of a clockwork motor. Looking up where a thunder-cloud ought to have been she saw instead a chin both modest and manly which was trying hard to look like the chin of her future husband.

'Where am I?' she murmured unnecessarily, but with a sense that the words were proper to so incredible and serene a situation in which the entire forest seemed vibrant with the relief of being alive.

'In my lap,' said Ernest, with prosaic exactitude. He put away the benzedrine inhaler and smoothed back the rioting of her hair from her forehead. She lay there looking up at him. Her eyes were forest eyes with a soft, startled lustre under which the brilliance glowed rather than shone.

'You're beautiful,' he said to the depths of those eyes.

'Thank you, Ernest,' she said. 'I'll always believe you when I hear you say that.'

'You've got that special pulled-out-of-the-lake look.'

'And you've got that life-saving air about your chin. Did you come to Mudalur just to save me, Ernest?'

'Don't flatter yourself,' he said. 'I'm not going to say I haven't missed you, or that I'd have personally made the trip up from Arkayam if I hadn't remembered that you lived at the end of the line. But I've other reasons for being in this country. Malaria *is* my speciality and it's India's biggest problem.'

'So it isn't a coincidence that you should end up here.'

'Now that I'm here I'm going to take you away from all this.'

'I'm very grateful,' she said, 'but I've no intention of leaving.'

'Don't tell me you're happy in this mud-bath.'

'It isn't a question of happiness.'

'Don't give me that stuff about duty and responsibility.'

She had pulled a leaf over her face and he flicked it off abruptly.

'Stop playing,' he said. 'Stop trying to confuse yourself with the foliage. You don't belong in this mess of vegetation.'

'And where am I supposed to belong?' she demanded. 'On top of stiletto heels in a split-level home? With a kitchen tailored to match my lingerie?'

'You're not being fair,' he said. 'The truth about us isn't in that kind of smartness.'

'Then the truth about us isn't in our poverty, either.'

He was quick to concede the point. 'You're absolutely right, Nell. But don't pretend that you don't know what I mean. You were happy in America. You were part of the place and yet completely yourself in it, and you made everything around you a little more real by being there. Don't you sometimes feel that you'd like to go back?'

'Of course,' she said. 'I feel it often and deeply enough to hurt. I can't ever forget what I've found among you, the freedom and the security, the wheels in the subway telling you that you matter and the glow of discovering that you belong to yourself and aren't owned by a lot of obligations that came into existence before you were even born. I like your houses because they're vivid and new and haven't been built with memories, because you can look through wide windows that aren't barred, on to front lawns that contain all of one's happiness.'

'I wish I could take you off that lotus,' he said. 'If you go on much longer you're going to make me home-sick.'

'I don't want it to be more than a dream.'

'Reach up and you can make it real.'

'I don't want to,' she repeated. 'Not that I'm scared of happiness. Don't smile; some of my people are. Sometimes you feel you're watched over by the shadows, you're frightened by the poverty, hemmed in by the emptiness and you want suddenly to scream for all the lights to be switched on. It's overwhelming and you want to lock yourself out of it. But then you begin to feel a sense of peace – not happiness at all, but something rarer; you've got to feel a little frightened at first for that kind of peace to drop into your being. A place like this is absurd and obstinate, the people believe in outrageous legends and you feel that you can't possibly resign yourself to their idiocy. Then you sing a

song that's nearly as old as the hills and suddenly the shape
of the hills makes it real. You realise that you were born
here just as the song was.'

'I understand,' he said. 'Is that a very Hindu way of
saying you'd rather not marry me?'

'You're attracted to me when I am drowning,' she said.
'If I were high and dry I mightn't look the same to you.'

He stiffened a little. 'I was asking to marry you and not
your predicament.'

'I know that,' she said. 'But circumstances are important
too. They change what people are and what they think
they're capable of doing. I'd like to see you change the
landscape not just in my own life, but in the lives of thousands of others. It's what you were intended for. You've
got this impatience to improve things which everyone jokes
about and without which everything would be so much
more meaningless. So you must resign yourself to your fate.
It's un-American to go on thinking of saving me. You've
got to think of saving whole communities.'

'I could marry you and do that also,' he said, 'in a sort of
combined undertaking. It's just the proposition for someone young and dynamic.'

'Now don't be too ambitious,' she reproved him. 'You're
going to marry someone who's sensible and functional.
She'll have a thirty-six, twenty-four, thirty-six figure.
Coming or going, she'll always look the same to you.
She'll remind you of convertibles. I'm being mean about
her because I'm jealous about her already. But marry her
and go home to her.'

She was out of his lap and had propped herself up on her

elbows. Though she was looking away from him, he could see that her eyes were not as bright as the phrases.

'As you like, Nell,' he said. 'We'll come back to reality. Do you realise that there's a nasty-looking bruise upon your left arm?'

'Is there?' she said, almost indifferently.

'And your beautiful clothes are very nearly ruined.'

She nearly jumped out of her sari when she heard that.

'You're mean,' she said. 'You should have told me as soon as I woke up. It's my eighth-best georgette I'm wearing. Here we've been wasting time talking about the future and all the while the stain has been eating into the cloth.'

'I'm sorry,' he said, smiling. 'We'll do what we can to fix it.'

'And are my eyes red as evil into the bargain?'

'They're as clear as Hindu philosophy. They're as luminous as the truths you've just been unfolding.'

She sighed. 'I suppose that means I'd better wash them. Could you help me to the stream, please, Ernest? To that rock at the edge of the water?'

He carried her in his arms and lowered her gently on to it. She took her slippers off and put them beside her. Her movements were angular and almost childlike. Then she dangled her feet in the gently swirling water and proceeded to wash the border of her sari with an absorbed intentness that seemed not to withdraw her but rather to reach out of her so that her presence merged into the surrounding tranquillity. The heat over the forest was dense and crushing, a curtain of inertness through which the sun had to struggle, throwing on her skin the blurring, blending

tracery of the entangled and unmoving trees. Her hair leapt
down upon her, drenching her fine-boned shoulders,
imprisoning in its turbulence the quietness of her face,
which seemed returned to itself, composed and vivid, not
so much seeing as silently receiving. She was too civilised
to be truly a creature of the forest, but she remained real,
a lustre in its shadows absorbing and giving back the
quality of the place. He sat down on the bank close by
her; she was unaware of his presence. She washed her face
in her cupped hands, and the water clung to her, spangling
upon her, catching its own gleam from the translucence of
her skin, under which the darkness glowed like the warmth
of the earth. He looked at her directly and steadily, but
she did not see him. She was part of the trance of the place.
He laid his hands on her shoulders. She neither trembled
nor sought to withdraw. Her eyes were serene, reproach-
less and confidently watchful. All of a sudden he could see
nothing but himself in them. The peace of her presence
passed gently into him so that his fingers did not drop
away but quietly relaxed. He must have smiled because her
smile had the quality of an answer, reflecting what he felt
and giving it stability.

He let his hands drape her hair behind her shoulders.
Her necklace was askew and he rearranged it with an
impersonal tenderness. She had drawn up her legs on the
rock and as she sat curled upon it, her hair, tumbling across
it, seemed to have grown out of its crevices, so that she was
the spell of the stone, the confession and inward chant of
its nature. He began to see the purpose of all those third-
rate pictures of Hindu deities, ruminating on boulders or

heavily poised upon lotuses, against a background of admiring cows or attentive elephants half immersed in oceans of milk. The girl in front of him made sense of all the trash. Watching her, he had a conviction of contentment, a sense of finding something precisely and purely itself. She was the reality and reason of the place. The grace of her body was vivid as it had to be, and yet in that flash of perception almost inanimate, so that she seemed truly to have sung her way out of the stone. Yet he knew that the reality could not last, that when the clarity passed and the thread of intensity was broken she would draw back to her ordinary nature. If he rubbed his eyes, she would disappear like all visions, or be changed into a mantis or a lizard, or a confusion of light in the pool of the rock's shadow. So he didn't rub his eyes. Instead he moved forward and kissed her, and that made it clear that all he was seeing was real and that nothing in it would ever need to be changed.

She didn't move yet. He was glad that the picture hadn't been dissolved by his intrusion into it. He stepped back to look at her, and now he was able to see past her to the road and the jeep and the dented rim of the D.D.T. drum with its off-white smudges.

'I'm sorry,' he said. 'It was too much like a dream. I shouldn't have touched it. I ought to have pinched myself instead.'

She held her hand out to him. Her face still had that intense and distant tranquillity which might perhaps prevail a moment longer before the pulse of the everyday came back to animate it. She was smiling at him, but only with her voice.

178

'Mr Jones,' she said, 'you'll have to show me the way back.'

He took her down the slope and he knew that she would always know the way back, whoever took her hand or discovered herself in her eyes, whatever other picture she walked into, gilded and garlanded by her fond, blundering parents.

'Would you marry me,' he asked, 'if I was Indian and our horoscopes agreed? The real ones, I mean. Not the ones you made up at Lake Placid.'

'Why then,' she said, 'you'd be a different person.'

'Well, would you marry that person?'

'I couldn't really tell until I'd met him, could I?'

'Supposing your parents hated him?'

'Then I'd marry him at once.'

'Not to protect him from being poisoned?'

'Definitely not,' she said. 'Only because of the look in his eyes.'

She had wiggled into the jeep and he sat down beside her. He let the clutch in tenderly as if he were the chauffeur of a Rolls Royce. Ten minutes later he slammed hard on the brakes. Lakshmi was standing across the track, glaring at them like an avenging deity, her fists raised towards the thunder-filled heavens.

'There he is!' she screamed. 'Horse-whip that lascivious cowboy.'

'I'm afraid I can't,' said Sambasivan unhappily. 'You see, I don't possess a horse-whip. And Kesavan won't be able to design one. It can't be found in the Sears Roebuck catalogue.'

IV

That afternoon the sun made one of its rare appearances. Everyone who was working stopped immediately to look at this phenomenon. The two children who had been born since the rains came were brought out and gurgled happily at the glittering ball which seemed to be so much more radiant than their fathers. The village historian consulted his records and informed everyone that nothing like this had ever before happened on the second of July. The village Jeremiah predicted that this shocking event could mean only the beginning of the deluge.

Raman pulled a hair out of his chest, came out of his hut and breathed the air suspiciously. He hung his strop across the entrance. Ten feet in length and butter-soft in texture, it was, beyond question, the finest strop in India. It reminded Raman of a whip. One day he would scourge iniquity with its proceeds. At the moment he sharpened his razor on it, sensitively, caressingly, like a virtuoso tuning his favourite instrument. The edge glittered at him and he stared back at it gloomily. In all the six years that he had owned that razor he had not cut even the throat of a chicken with it. His theoretical education had been perfect; his heart thudded angrily with the sense of humanity wronged; his eyes flashed messianically and conviction glowed in his voice when he called on the down-trodden to rise and recover their heritage. The thought of violence filled him with reforming exaltation; the sight of it invariably made him sick.

He had felt like this ever since that evening in his childhood when he wandered past the huts by the reeking canal and the squealing, desperate pig had charged out, flinging him headlong into the slimy water. The blood had spattered on him from the gash in its neck. Behind it were six men determined to dine on roast pork. They had not even noticed him. They threw a net round the pig and hauled it back. He clambered half-way up the bank and lay there trembling, listening to the animal's screams. When he could stand it no longer he got up and stumbled towards them. They were convulsed with laughter by his appeals at first; then they became angry and showered blows upon him with their sandals. He retreated, but he couldn't run away. He stood there watching the fire leap and the cruelty flash in their faces, sickened by the babel of festivity through which the dying howls of the animal ebbed till the last thick gasp had sucked at the pit of his fear. Then he fled as fast as he could and arrived home breathless and sobbing. He was too upset even to tell his story, so his parents beat him for having ruined his clothes.

The next day was cripplingly hot. The wind was a furnace scorching his eyeballs, clinging to his skin, leeching the strength out of his dejected body. Even the asphalt on the road was melting. His limbs ached from the previous night's punishment so that he could hardly push the pedals of his bicycle. It was a perfect day for selling ice-cream. He had been selling it for nine months, but never in such quantities. He forced himself panting, up driveway after driveway, to the cool, secluded, tree-darkened homes of the rich, dispensing the cones and scoops and chocolate-covered sandwiches, watching the nectar dribble down the children's gleeful faces while he fidgeted barefooted on the blistering cutting gravel. He had never tasted a single scoop himself. Each time after the feast by proxy had ended, he would pull out his book and scrupulously add up the accounts for every mouthful. Then he would salaam obsequiously, wheel his machine to the gate and push his pedals into the next frustration. The remembrance of their laughter thickened in his throat. It became the recurring taunt of a world beyond him, stabbing down relentlessly into the daze of his thirstiness. He had asked for water once and they had emptied a *cooja* on the ground in front of him.

At three o'clock in the evening he could stand it no longer. He pushed his machine under the shade of a tamarind tree, flung open the ice-box and made up for nine months of deprivation with ten celestial scoops of strawberry flavour. Then he lay down in a profound and intoxicated peace and slumbered soundly on top of his account book. When he awoke it was too late for remorse. His employer's shop had shut an hour ago and the alarm must have already been sounded. He did the natural thing and went home; he could not have been more unwise. The slum where he lived had never heard of ice-cream, and hordes of children followed him like the Pied Piper, capering delightedly round the strange contraption which Raman pedalled dazedly to disaster. When he reached the entrance of his house, his employer was already there, panting with the exertions of his preliminary war-dance. His father Natesan was looking for a weapon of assault while roaring bellicosely about the honour of his house. His mother,

unnerved by the menaces, had produced a form in tripli-
cate which she was imploring everyone to fill up. Into this
pandemonium Raman was propelled, sin-stained and straw-
berry-besotted, unable to retreat through the half-naked
ranks behind him. The two men, seeing the miscreant,
buried the hatchet and fell on the source of their dissension
with a strap. When justice had been done Natesan retired
to the bedroom and there proceeded to chastise his wife for
having reared so unnatural an offspring. His wrath
appeased, he staggered again to the entrance, drained of
his strength and exhausted of his income. Raman had been
the family's only wage-earner. The knowledge that he
would have to choose between starving or working drove
Natesan into further tantrums and to a furious lecture on
the injustice of Providence to an unnerved audience of
cows, cats and children.

As for Raman, he retired into the latrine, that being the
place where deadly oaths were sworn, and setting his thumb
tearfully against his nose he vowed that he would never
rest until he had achieved a social order in which every child
living could have his fair lick of the spoon. Then he lay
down to rest as far from his father as possible and in the
dead of night ran away, not forgetting to take with him
the contents of the cash-box. His progress after that had
been tortuous, but the burning sense of injustice remained
to guide him. He had begged for some time; then he became a cobbler's assistant. From mending slippers he proceeded to licking them; then disgusted by his own servility,
he spent a year in jail for eloquently saying the right things
at the wrong moment. Prison gave him the opportunity to

meditate and, like many men who think, his thoughts turned to destruction. But he was no push-button revolutionary. He wanted passionately to be able to choose his own pig and to roast it. If he came to Mudalur it was because no one could take it from him. There was something about the place which cried out for annihilation; it was so removed from reality, so sunk in the slough of its lunacy, seduced by an outrageous legend of mangoes, abandoned by heaven and bypassed by history. From the moment he saw it he felt that characteristic thrill of disgust which he knew was the assertion of his divine right to transform. He would burn out the corruption of apathy at its heart. He would stamp upon it the vigour of his pure zeal for revolution.

Yet he knew that this could never be so, even before the quicksands seized him and drew him down into that stupefied tranquillity which the rains curtained and the forests protected and the unchanging clouds of delusion eddied over. He was accustomed to indifference; he was born to speak to stone and to make the wells of despondency ring with the truth. However deep the hopelessness, he had the power to agitate it, to make it seethe with his anger and the strength of his vision of change. Yet he shrank from the forces which he lusted to let loose. His mind called out for the trampling of the demon, the onrush of the deluge, for the dance of destruction that was the instrument of renewal. Yet his nerves winced away from the screams of the animal, the sting of his father's lash and the sense of dizziness that seemed to seize him when, however mildly, he nicked a customer under his chin. He was poised forever on a razor's edge. He would never be able to take history by the throat. All he could do was to invite it into a chair and give it a haircut.

Possessed by this ambivalence, he strummed the razor dementedly against the inviting, everlasting length of the strop. It was right that he should be a barber. A barber could learn much if he kept his own mouth shut and did not too clumsily shut the mouths of others. He sat at the centre of omniscience, at the hub of the cartwheel of change. The knife was in his hand and the execution beckoned beyond it whenever he could screw his blood-thirstiness to the sticking point, above the threshold of the screaming.

With a savage gesture, he seized the ancient bottle of Château Yquem which now contained Murugesan's Non-Violent, High-Fidelity Shaving Compound. No one, not even Murugesan, knew quite how the concoction was made, but it produced what was required, namely lather, in foaming abundance. Raman threw a handful of it into the pot of water upon the fire. It bubbled and seethed like a cauldron of iniquity. As he stirred it his vanishing hopes returned. Atlantis was drowned, Sodom lay under the ashes, Babylon, that great city, was fallen, fallen and the days of the sandalwood house were also numbered.

A voice twanged in his ear like the sudden snapping of a thread of fate. He whipped around. It was the recurrent nightmare in khaki pants with that horrible, purposive look upon his face as if the world were bound to get steadily better.

'Say,' said Ernest. 'Don't tell me that you're the barber around here.'

185

Raman glared at him disdainfully. 'All my work is done strictly by appointment.'

'I'd like an appointment,' said Ernest. 'Right now. Since you don't seem to be doing anything but thinking.'

He sat down on the packing-case to which Raman waved, straightened his long legs and leaned back against the thatched side of the hut, which swayed dangerously with the weight of his body.

'Is it true, like they say, that you don't really belong in Muddle Ore?'

'I've just as much right to be here as anyone else.'

'But you're not a genuine native?'

'I came here last year,' said Raman. 'I live in the place because I can't stand the sight of it.'

'That's like it should be,' Ernest said approvingly. 'If you hate something real bad then you begin to want to change it.'

'Not in the way you think.'

'If we want the same things we're liable to think the same way. You believe in progress, don't you?'

'I believe in independence.'

'And you're in favour of a world without malaria?'

'I'd prefer one without foreigners.'

'We're the same,' said Ernest. 'Under the arguments we can't help being the same. I got my doubts and you got your suspicions. Let's liquidate them in a common programme.'

Liquidation was about what Raman wanted. He leaped on the brush and plunged it into the cauldron. His victim's face was immersed in clouds of lather.

'It's a real nice day,' gurgled Ernest.

'How true,' said Raman. 'I doubt very much if you will see another one like it.'

Ernest twisted apprehensively as the razor swooped down. He need not have been anxious. From the moment that the blade touched his victim's Adam's apple Raman felt his familiar restraining tingle of horror. The sense of impotence rippled up his fingers. The desire to kill and the shuddering distaste for killing balanced each other in that tension of fluent movement which was the humiliating source of his talents as a barber. He shaved smoothly and, to the spectator, fervently, with a frustrated, finely-controlled finesse that in a more populous place than Mudalur might have brought him renown and a vitreous enamel basin. The lather was cleared from the upper lip in two swift, delicate flicks; the chin was dealt with in a single sweep that skidded dashingly over the cleft at its centre. In less time than it takes to broil a lobster, Ernest had been done without a nick. Raman stepped back, surveyed his handiwork and snorted with disgust. Ernest got to his feet, still a little surprised at his good fortune, smelling uncharacteristically of menthol and aged sauterne.

'Keep the change,' he said generously, handing Ramon two silver rupees.

Raman flung the money back at him. 'See if you can buy yourself popularity with it.'

A frown creased the saddle-leather smoothness of Ernest's face.

'You don't seem to like me,' he concluded acutely. 'So since you've nothing more important to do, let's get together and try to figure it out. I'm optimistic, I guess, but I can't help thinking that once we've sized up and ironed out our differences we've got to achieve a real meeting of minds. Take the weight off your feet, friend, and tell the world what's eating you.'

'It's your blasted triviality,' Raman exploded, impotently flourishing his razor. 'You think that to change the world you need only to disinfect it. Spray everything with Flit, give everyone an injection, buy them new clothes with which to call on prosperity and they all have to be like you, reading the same trash and gaping at the same movies. You're a diversionist and a saboteur. You don't mean any harm, I suppose, but objectively you're an enemy of history.'

Ernest stuck to his position. 'The only difference is poverty. And the only problem that matters is how we're going to get rid of it.'

'So if we were rich enough we'd all of us be American.'

'What's wrong with that?' asked Ernest.

'Nothing as far as you are concerned,' said Raman.' It's one way of being alive. I've no objection to your being your-self in America. But not in Mudalur. We don't want your hygiene. Blood must flow. The pillars of tyranny have to be made to topple. The people have to be scourged to set them-selves free and you come here in your damned jeep bringing them balm and bandages. They're supposed to wipe out oppression, not mosquitoes. You're a menace to them. You're a salesman of dangerous sedatives. Objectively, you are a per-nicious dilettante, All you can do is shave the face of events!'

He stopped in his peroration, abruptly conscious of the razor in his hand. In the shining blade he saw himself and the reflection of his remarks. He turned back to Ernest with forced calm.

'Now that I've clarified your treason to the future, would you kindly cease to infest my house?'

'Gee,' said Ernest with innocent cruelty. 'It must be eating you bad. You sound like a kid that's never had any ice-cream.'

He put his hands in his pockets and left, whistling. Raman watched him going down the hill. It was not too late to leap on him and to stab him in the back. There were better ways to kill a man of course, but the point was to kill somebody sometime. He brandished the razor menacingly in a final effort to provoke himself and saw his eyes flush with animal fury in it. With a shiver of frustration he put it down on the packing-case and, sighing heavily, turned back to his cauldron.

Why was it, he asked himself with dejected bitterness, that all foreigners irresistibly reminded him of pigs?

v

In fact there was more than one way to stab a foreigner and the preparations had begun well before Ernest's arrival. The first man to have his hair cut on that unnatural afternoon had gone up the slope immediately after his prayers. When the ordeal was over he came down and said them again. What was hissed into his ear had confirmed his worst suspicions. He called for his wife, locked her up with the cattle in the cowshed and stood outside with arms folded and a death-dealing look. To his curious colleagues he spat out his reasons. Their faces grew grim and they also secured their chattels. The facts were indeed no less than they had expected. There could be only one conclusion about what had happened in the forest and that conclusion soon hardened into anger against the uninvited foreigner who professed weird aims to cover familiar vices. The procession of clients to the hut on the hill steadily lengthened. It was a wonderful day for a haircut; and besides, the news was sinful enough to remove the dandruff from any customer's scalp. Clots of scandal began to form and to ferment; the details of dishonour, poured dexterously in, seethed in the ears of Raman's visitors, like Murugesan's lather on their faces.

The day was unprecedented and the sun shone brilliantly, but it did not smile on the success of Ernest's work. In other places the response had sometimes been cautious, but the villagers had always been able first to grasp and then to demand what was plainly in their interests. Often no propaganda was necessary. People knew of the malarial land that had been reclaimed, of the sterile acres made green for cultivation, of people who for the first time were able to work in their own fields, who were hands to produce as well as mouths to be fed. Mudalur had been reached late; spraying normally ceased before the rainy season; but here was an unsuspected pocket of infection which had to be dealt with if the campaign was to succeed. He had to move on, to take advantage of the break in the weather, yet he was acutely conscious that he was getting nowhere. Wherever he went the doors were bolted to him. The day was inauspicious; the wife of the tenant was pregnant; the owner of the hut was in Arkayam, unable to return, and his son had no power to authorise repairs to its fabric. One man had malaria already; another had entered a state of union with the infinite and his hard-won equilibrium could not be disturbed. The excuses were untidy and hastily concocted; the people, instinctively courteous to strangers, were still reluctant to say what they actually thought; but underneath the evasions Ernest was increasingly aware of the resentful looks and the hardening hostility.

In the house Nalini was not being any more successful. Three hours in the jungle was a difficult thing to explain.

'The engine broke down,' she said. 'You saw it happen yourself.'

'And what was supposed to be wrong with it?'

'There were centipedes in the insides.'

'And it took three hours to find them, did it? The man's an American, isn't he? At the very least he should be a mechanical genius.'

'After the centipedes there was the elephant.'

'Elephant,' snorted Lakshmi. 'Are you perfectly sure that that is what you saw?'

'Of course I'm sure,' said Nalini. 'It was sweet and awkward and it had such appealing eyes.'

'And what went on after that?'

'I fed it bananas and then I fell on my back.'

Lakshmi whipped round on Sambasivan. 'That's what comes of a foreign education.'

'We offered her as a maiden,' her husband said. 'I'm afraid the advertisement is out of date.'

'As if that matters,' wailed Lakshmi.

'I agree,' said Sambasivan. 'There's no point now in issuing a corrigendum.'

'But nothing happened,' Nalini protested.

'Don't try to deceive me, wretched girl. You're looking twice as beautiful as yesterday. It's absolute proof that you've been up to no good.'

'But, Mother, you're just imagining things. It's all so simple and straightforward. I fell down after the elephant chased us. And then I inhaled some benzedrine. And then I sat on a rock and Ernest looked at me for ten minutes.'

'You call him Ernest, eh?'

'Of course, Mother. You've heard me do it yourself. After all I *have* known him for years.'

'And all he did was look at you?'

'Well, now that you remind me, he also arranged my necklace.'

'It's impossible,' said Lakshmi. 'Either he's a fool or you're a liar.'

'Well, Mr Jones is a most unusual person.'

'My poor child, there's no question of being unusual. It's perfectly plain what happened. Your hair's in a mess. Your sari is torn in all the obvious places. And, to cap it all, there's that shocking bruise on your left arm where this monster held you in his hot embraces.'

'What nonsense,' said Nalini. 'If he clutches anything like that it's his precious camera. He'd never dream of doing that to me.'

'Desire,' said Sambasivan, 'takes no account of decent intentions. I am obliged to agree with your mother. If you remember nothing it is because you were not meant to. The benzedrine was clearly chloroform.'

'This is what your folly has led to,' Lakshmi cried, shaking her fist operatically at her husband. 'My home invaded and my daughter ravished; by a worm who comes here pretending to kill insects. This is what your advertisement has brought us.'

'But, my dear, he didn't answer the advertisement. He's an international civil servant here on official business. You might call him a bridegroom of lost causes.'

'So my daughter is a lost cause now.'

'If you were to trumpet that less loudly we might still get her married.'

'Married to what, may I ask? To a lobster-faced American. He doesn't even possess a frigidaire. And he drives a second-hand jeep instead of a decent Plymouth.'

'I'm sick of this drivel,' Nalini said, stamping her foot. 'There's nothing, absolutely nothing, wrong with me. If you don't believe that, go and consult a doctor.'

'And what do you expect us to do then?' her father asked. 'Do we proudly nail his certificate to the sun-dial? My dear child, it isn't sin that matters, it's the appearance of sin. You were in the jungle and you were alone for three hours. If you did what you shouldn't have, that's deplorable. If you didn't, that's even worse, it's unnatural. I see no alternative but to double your dowry.'

'Much good that is,' grumbled Lakshmi. 'My accounts show clearly that two times nothing is nothing.'

'But beauty is infinite,' said Sambasivan gallantly.

'Indeed it is,' Lakshmi retorted. 'And in case you've forgotten, folly is also endless.'

'You're both impossible,' Nalini said, half in tears. She went out, dabbing at her face with her handkerchief. At the entrance she bumped into Visvakarman.

'Don't marry him,' he counselled. 'It is not necessary. In modern India we are able to be broad-minded.'

'You can stuff your proposal back into that filthy mind of yours.'

He stiffened, characteristically. 'My offer was made solely in your interests. All he wants is a garage mechanic. Marry me and you can be a typist instead.'

He noticed the tears beginning to come to her eyes.

'You are crying,' he said, observantly. 'Collect yourself, if you please. It is not right to be overwhelmed by my kindness. A Hindu wife should be unchanging in misery and in good fortune.'

'I'll never marry you,' she screamed. 'Not even if you were to leave at once for another planet. I'd be able to smell your smugness even from there. I'd rather clean sewers than wash up your dishes. I'd rather wait hand and foot for the rest of my life on the illegitimate offspring of a toad and a weasel.'

'Your Billingsgate is remarkable,' he exclaimed. 'Content of course is not to be expected. But you, it appears, can be both fishwife and housewife. An unusual combination, provided it is disciplined. I have not seen it in the modern Indian novel.'

She brushed past him and ran out of the house. Her father followed her. For the first time his tone was peremptory.

'You will confine yourself to your room, as far as possible. And make no attempt to communicate with Dr Jones. Trouble is stirring. You are the cause of it even if you are innocent. Be sure you do nothing to worsen the situation.'

She had to retreat to her window. Outside, the village was seething. The barber's hut was an anthill of activity. Raman's eyes flashed and his smile became more and more handsomely diabolical as he fed the commotion from the height of his triumph. The foreigner was a locust. He had come to lay waste new acres. How could it be assumed that the complicated machines he had brought with him were intended merely to eliminate mosquitoes? The tubes and nozzles were meant for a more sinister purpose. As for the so-called D.D.T., its evil significance should by now be self-evident so that any moron could comprehend what was sprayed on his wall. Raman's audience listened enraptured to him, curious at first, then shocked and finally convinced of Ernest's depravity by the gargantuan character of his misdeeds. The rhythm of disgust began to strengthen. Threatening voices were heard above the hisses and hums of dismay. Indignation grew steadily against the gangling foreigner with his infernal instruments who, it was now obvious, had made his trip to India because he was too depraved even for the lascivious West.

Raman held up his hands. The forest of voices around him grew suddenly still. He mounted the crate on which his customers normally sat and looked triumphantly into the mirror of his audience. He proceeded to pour oil on the waters he had troubled.

'We must beware of jumping to conclusions.'

'Who's jumping?' a voice asked. 'The facts speak for themselves. Everything is as clear as if I saw it with my own eyes.'

'Perhaps the three hours in the forest were spent in admiring tropical fauna. After all the man has unusual tastes.'

'Unusual indeed. The only thing that's unusual about this business is his having to come ten thousand miles to do it.'

'And lecturing everyone else on public health.'

'We ought to souse him in his own insecticides.'

'You have decided wisely,' Raman said. 'Now you must be magnanimous. To understand is also to forgive.'

'Forgive, indeed! What's the matter with you, young Raman?'

'For making Mudalur a laughing stock?'

'For polluting our homes with his medicines?'

'No woman will be safe until he's locked up.'

Raman's hands moved in a lyrical arc as if he were silencing an orchestral crescendo or shaving the customer of his dreams.

'We must consider him objectively. He is not just an individual monstrosity but the product of a decadent social order. It is not enough to remove him. We must purge ourselves of the values he represents.'

'Excellently put,' a mellow voice said. Raman's head jerked back as he recognised the familiar word. Kubera advanced towards him flourishing his Patek Phillippe watch to make it evident that the hour had struck.

'He is right,' he said to the crowd. 'The impresario of the razor is right. We are united in essentials. Our common interest is the welfare of Mudalur.'

'Not through your obscene superstitions,' Raman said warningly.

Kubera patted him on the back. 'My dear friend, don't make the mistake of confusing morals with politics. Let us destroy what we agree on destroying first. Then we can think of destroying each other afterwards.'

'Very well,' said Raman, after some hesitation. 'I am prepared to form a popular front. But I want it to be clear that I intend to cut your throat thoroughly after Hamilton Jones and Sambasivan are ruined.'

'The future will decide that,' Kubera said, blandly.

'The future will make dust of vermin like you.'

'Tush, tush!' said Kubera. 'You must not disturb our newly-created harmony. This is my proposal,' he continued, raising his voice so that the crowd could hear him. 'Mudalur has been desecrated by our unwanted and wanton guest. It is our sacred duty to expel him. But before we can do so we must rid our minds of his influence. We can only hope to destroy successfully if the spirit of destruction is serene and disinterested. This it cannot be as long as our hearts remain clouded by natural emotions. Fortunately, tomorrow is the day of the expedition. Let us gather the mangoes and renew ourselves in their holiness. Then with our minds centred on ultimate truth we can eliminate the lustful American and his over-zealous host.'

'I disagree!' cried Raman. 'The time to act is now. Let us strike while the iron is hot and our anger is mobilised.'

'There is no possibility of the iron cooling. We are isolated by the American's rashness. None of us can escape. Consequently we can strike whenever we wish. There is no need to act hastily and to prejudice our cause by lack of organisation. Time is on our side. By doing nothing for the time being we can lull our victim into a false sense of security. Tomorrow the mangoes will be gathered, the night will be one of celebration and nothing but gaiety will be expected from us. If the blow falls it will be crushing and conclusive.'

Raman squirmed angrily. He realised that Kubera knew what he wanted and that he was determined to set aside any distractions between him and his objective. All Mudalur must be absorbed by the expedition, pledged to its promises, intoxicated by the dreams it held out. If violence took place it would have to take place after that. It was not certain that it would take place even then. New alliances could be formed after the full moon: Kubera and the American; Kubera and Nalini. Anything could come out of this mango mumbo-jumbo. He scented treachery but he could do nothing to prevent it. Kubera had the magic formula: money to begin with and miracles to follow. All Raman could offer was sweat, tears and a blood-bath.

Still, two could play at the game of power politics. Bemused by bribes, delirious with the smell of success, Kubera's followers seemed to have forgotten that the mountain was difficult and in monsoon conditions dangerous. The expedition would fail. Disaster would strike it. The future would belong to doom and the deluge. Raman's eyes glinted at the thought and he had to restrain himself consciously from executing a preliminary caper in the dance of destruction.

'I have no objection to your expedition,' he said. 'But what is to follow must follow. Let everyone here recognise that our common platform is the necessity of violence. That which is evil must be wiped out for ever.'

'Certainly,' said Kubera. 'I stand for a radically new order, a complete break with the unfortunate past of this village.' He held his hand out to Raman in a platitudinous gesture.

The crowd cheered mildly at the success of this miniature summit meeting. Kubera acknowledged the applause and waddled off. Even his back looked successful, Raman thought, bitterly.

The sun had set. The air began to sing in the gathering darkness. Stepping into the circles of the sandalwood house, Kubera hummed happily to himself.

'Any news?' Sambasivan asked, a trifle anxiously.

'I am afraid my efforts at moderation have failed.'

Sambasivan sighed. 'That means another one of my durbars. Let's hope I can talk a little sense into them.'

'I'd advise you to lie low and to refrain from speeches. Leave everything to me. Though I cannot prevent the crisis I am confident that I can postpone it for a few days. By that time, the American army of liberation will have arrived and you and he will be able to depart without danger.'

He looked around the house like an auctioneer.

'This place is quite worthless,' he said. 'However, since I greatly dislike bargaining I shall make you an offer that is unnecessarily generous. Ten thousand rupees including the furniture, grounds and livestock.'

'I'm sorry,' said Sambasivan, 'I've no intention of leaving.'

'I advise you not to stay. If you insist on doing so, your property will be destroyed. If you leave it will remain more or less intact even though it will no longer be your property. I cannot live in it of course, but with some redecoration it could be made into a warehouse. Your exile need not be permanent: people have short memories and within five years you can probably return as my caretaker. Unfortunately, I can do nothing for your daughter. I am liberal about these things, but Cæsar's wife has to be free from scandal. The same is fortunately not true of Cæsar's cook.'

'It's no use my explaining,' Sambasivan said. 'I'm getting old and I've always been obstinate and my wife isn't the only one who thinks I'm weak in the head. But this place has grown up around me. All its mistakes are part of me. I've got identified with it in a way I can't expect you to understand. But I'm sure you *will* understand my refusing to convey your last proposal to Lakshmi.'

Kubera smiled confidently. 'You need not trouble. The future will see to that. I have always found the future most co-operative.'

He turned to the door. 'I have to go now. It is time to observe the progress of the moon.'

He went out. It was a night of voluptuous darkness against which the diamond-hard stars shone almost fiercely. The moon was just rising, silvering the rim of the hills. Kubera watched the spectacle without seeing it. Then he became conscious of somebody else beside him.

'You are interested in the heavens, Mr Jones?'

'Not really,' Ernest said. 'But after today's mess there's a feeling of peace in all this.'

'I understand. I have heard the talk in the village.'

'There isn't an atom of truth in it.'

'Exactly! It's an illusion. And what does that prove? That only illusions work. That the people live upon them. To-morrow. I shall prove that for the greater good of Mudalur.'

'I hope you don't really mean that,' Ernest said.

'You are an American so you are matter-of-fact. This is a different world. If you are fed you are fortunate. To prosper is miraculous. You cannot keep on enduring it without a sign from the sky.'

'Show the people what's good for them and they'll always be ready to fight for it.'

'Your method has failed.'

'Because of a misunderstanding.'

'It would never have succeeded,' Kubera said. 'What can you offer? That if they follow you faithfully they won't suffer from something that most of them haven't got. That their children's children will eat more and live longer. I am more practical. I give them *tamasha* and miracles. I tell them that the supernatural is on their side. To believe in yourself is not enough in these mountains. It is always better to march with the supernatural.'

'Particularly if there's a profit in it.'

Kubera shrugged his shoulders. 'That is surely of no consequence. What I take is taken only from what my methods give. Just as much as you, I am concerned over Mudalur's welfare. I supported your health programme. It is a pity that your behaviour has ruined it.'

'It's tough luck,' Ernest said. 'I'll need a miracle to put it back on the road.'

Kubera's eyes shone. 'Brilliantly put, my friend. Once you admit that there is always hope. Now let me think. There is no time to lose of course. The effect must be speedy and decisive. I have it, now I have it. Murugesan the treasurer is a pervert. He cackles obscenely whenever I offer him money. From the beginning he has opposed my expedition. So let us introduce a cobra into his hut. When it bites him you can treat him. If he dies it will prove conclusively that you cannot pour scorn on the legend of the mangoes. If he lives I shall let your medicines take the credit. However, you must promise that your subsequent miracles can be used for my purposes.'

Ernest eyed him incredulously. 'What kind of a person do you think I am? Down there they're denouncing me as a sex maniac. Up here you're trying to make me a murderer.'

'Then you don't approve of my plan?'

'I think it's disgusting and childish.'

'Very well,' said Kubera. 'I admit I thought of it on the spur of the moment. But don't stand there criticising, think of something more constructive. After all, it's only for your own good.'

'It must be the moon that's responsible,' Ernest said. He turned on his heel and walked into the house. Kubera made no attempt to follow. He could succeed without Ernest, without Raman. He had his finger on what the people wanted and could feel in his pulse the throb of his popularity.

He looked up. The night was glowingly dark like Nalini's hair. The moon shone on the landscape of the future with a discreet brilliance worthy of Cosmic Cosmetics. In the distance he could hear the chanting of voices as the preparations began for the morning's expedition.

He smiled benignly into the excellence of the night.

VI

THE DRUMS beat unceasingly in answer to everyone's headaches. Kubera had rounded-up every small boy in the neighbourhood and promised them prodigious quantities of sweets. They pounded away unmercifully with their home-made instruments of propitiation and assault as if they were pulverising the resistance of the mountain.

The village did not sleep and could not think. Those who were obstinate enough to close their eyes opened them as the commotion grew in intensity. They went out and rubbed them in the bedlam of the morning. Everywhere friezes of figures were capering through the mists towards the sagging *pandal* and the circular awning where Kubera stood at the centre of expectation, pontificating in his embroidered dhoti, his skin fat with rare oils, smeared with saffron and sandalwood paste and barricaded by marks of religion and dignity. The air was heavy with incense, the ground dewy with attar and with the petals of forest flowers, wilting from their vivid-ness. Under the intonings of the priests the green twigs were stacked high. Offerings of ghee were poured upon the pile from every household in the village. Fruit and vegetables were heaped around it. The fire was lit, the sticks sizzled and spluttered like Raman's rhetoric, the smoke billowed consolingly into everyone's eyes and the thanksgivings of the priests unrolled sonorously, patting all donors on their befuddled heads. Half the food reserves of the village were consumed dramatically in the blaze of holiness. The inhabi-tants of Mudalur watched the proceedings with nervous self-assurance like a man looking on and seeing his gold watch being systematically pulverised by a conjuror. They did not quite know how the redemption was to take place but they had given up enough for significance to follow. The *tamasha* was real and the truth must lie somewhere within it. They could see for themselves that where there was smoke there was fire and where there was fire there must presumably be holiness.

The blaze stilled, the gathering opened and a gust of fresh air swept in beneath the marquee. The intrepid mountaineers came forward. Their dhotis were starched and immaculate, their faces, under Raman's zealous razor, clean-shaven as a sacrificial morning. Proud of themselves, frightened a little by their own audacity, they bowed low to receive the blessing of the priests and the garlands showered upon them by their womenfolk. They rose, the music cascaded upon them, the improvised drums throbbed under the fists of the small boys and whatever remained of Mudalur's food was dispensed. Kubera seized the hand of the expedition's leader.

'Guruswami,' he said ringingly. 'Go forward to conquer like your ancestors.'

The man scratched one foot uncomfortably with the other.

'Well what are you waiting for? What's the matter with you?'

'Sahib, I shall do whatever the gods permit. But the mountain is rough and, as you see, I am barefoot.'

'Well, the *rishi* didn't have any slippers, did he? The top of the peak is holy. One usually enters a holy place without shoes.'

'I shall do as you insist, sahib. A poor man cannot afford to turn back from danger.'

'I am not aware of any danger,' Kubera said. 'All possible *mantrams* have been recited by the priests. And you will also be protected by your top hat.'

'But the hat was given to me for becoming a Christian.'

'Well, now that you're a Hindu again you must proceed to purify it. You cannot cart around your corrupt past on your head. Bring it back full of mangoes and wherever you go you will wear a halo of holiness.'

The man hesitated again. 'I put my faith in you, sahib,' he said, eventually. 'You are prosperous and so you must be honest. Otherwise, you would not be so blessed by the gods.'

'I guarantee results,' Kubera promised. 'Within a week of your climbing the peak, relief parties will arrive here from Arkayam. Your wife will discover riches unexpectedly in her back garden. You yourself will receive an offer of employment from Madura.'

The man's eyes widened. 'You foresee all this, sahib?'

'It is inevitable,' Kubera said. 'The mangoes cannot possibly do less.'

A murmur of expectation rippled through the gathering. The members of the expedition squared their shoulders. The drums gathered weight, the cries of farewell washed through the smoke as the climbers moved on through the village, followed first by their well-wishers, then only by children building mountains of dreams, till the mists rolled over them, their silhouettes growing fainter against a seething of loneliness into which the adventurers moved and were engulfed.

Kubera turned on his heel. 'I was sorry for the fellow,' he said to Sambasivan. 'But one must never make concessions in public. It's the thin end of the wedge and the beginning of inflation. In any case they can have prosperity to the extent that they deserve it. The mountain will give it to them – provided they work hard enough.'

'Quite,' said Sambasivan. 'That's an excellent pair of hob-nailed boots you're wearing.'

'It's a prudent precaution,' Kubera said. 'The path up to your house is sometimes treacherous. But that is a minor matter; there are more serious things to be done. Are the arrangements for my taking part in the expedition complete?'

'The telescope works,' Sambasivan said. 'I have also spoken solemnly to the clouds. But I doubt if I've been successful. They don't listen to me any more than the people of Mudalur.'

They had reached the house and he opened the door of the inner sanctum.

'You would like some coffee before commencing your vigil?'

'I think not,' Kubera said. 'I have a poor head for heights. I would not wish my self-indulgence to ruin the prospects of an entire expedition.'

Sambasivan looked appreciatively at him. He had no taste for the man, but, being an eccentric himself, he could not but admire so professional a performance.

'It's cold up there. Perhaps you'll need a blanket.'

'A very sound suggestion. Unlike my colleagues on the mountain, I haven't lived here and am not used to the climate.'

'And I can provide you with a first-rate first-aid kit.'

Kubera reared back nervously. 'Are you suggesting that I may meet with an accident?'

'Of course not. It's only a matter of prudence.'

'In that case provide me with a copy of the *Gita*. First-aid may be necessary for the spirit also.'

He squatted under the telescope and peered through the eyepiece.

'How about lunch?' Sambasivan asked, a trifle maliciously. 'Lakshmi is feeling tired after last night's commotion, so she has restricted herself to a modest menu of eight courses.'

Kubera's face set in an expression of resigned resolution.

'At twelve o'clock bring me a glass of spring water and half a dozen berries on a bay leaf.'

'Are you sure that is enough? It requires extra effort to climb with hob-nailed boots.'

'The strain of leadership takes away one's appetite.'

'I can't wish you success,' Sambasivan said, as he left, 'but it's more than my future is worth to wish you failure.'

He went out. Kubera closed and bolted the door, wrapped a woollen scarf solicitously round his neck, rubbed his hands, which were already becoming numb with the cold, and settled down to his share of the expedition. The climbers were still concealed in the clouds which had settled around the lower part of the peak, but Kubera had their timetable planned to a nicety. It was easy to follow their progress as he sweated and groaned up the formidable invisible slopes, shouting encouragement, cajoling and upbraiding, or gasping with horror at some particularly narrow escape. The mountain was below the snow-line and there was naturally no glacier on it; but that did not prevent his powerful imagination from falling into a crevasse. The minutes ticked by and the tension mounted. The berries brought into the room were ejected indignantly. Kubera fought for breath. He was overcome by the altitude. He complained piteously about the condition of his heart. Then a gurgle of triumph splashed messily through the concentric circles of Hillview as the facts took dizzy possession of his dreams and the expedition appeared in the field of view of the telescope, on the ridge above the clouds, vigorously and confidently climbing. Kubera clapped his hands and cried in ecstasy. He embraced the telescope, nearly demolishing the eyepiece. He pinned decorations on Guruswami's manly chest.

At twenty-seven minutes past one the keyhole audience absorbed in this performance heard a shriek of dismay, the sound of breaking glass and the unmistakable thud of a body falling. When they rushed in, Kubera was lying prostrate in an ooze of hair-oil. The blood had drained from his mahogany-coloured face leaving his complexion a mixture of clay and oatmeal.

'The first-aid kit,' he croaked.

Nalini snapped it open while Ernest felt his pulse.

'Not here, you fools. Up there. Do something quickly.'

They looked through the telescope and could see nothing. Then they swung it a little to the right and through the slur of the rain they were able to make out the slumped figures cautiously, dejectedly descending, carrying on their shoulder the limp, top-hatted body of their colleague.

VII

The storm was at its height when the expedition returned. Raman was ready to receive them. He was exultant and revengeful. The whole world was an extension of his condition.

They laid Guruswami down in the brick house that he

himself had built, the only one in the village apart from Hill-view. He lay there, moaning softly, looking at the wall and at his hands. His wife sat beside him, the tears streaming down her face. Then she dried them abruptly and stiffened herself into angry dignity,

'What else do you want to take from us?' Raman asked Nalini, who had limped into the room.

She looked around at the impassive, stony faces. She was drenched to the skin, but they seemed not to notice it. It must have been obvious that her ankle was hurting her, yet no one was prepared to ask her to sit down.

'I just want to help in any way that I can.'

'Don't delude yourself,' Raman said. 'Last-minute charities won't wipe out your guilt.'

She was becoming used to Raman's peculiar vision of the truth, but this latest development of it left her angry and incredulous.

'How can you possibly think of my being guilty? I've never heard anything so revoltingly fantastic.'

'You and your family are the cause of all this.'

'But you know very well that we had nothing to do with it – that we were against the whole scheme from the very beginning.'

'Yet you gave your hospitality to the man who invented it. You let him sit in your house and work out his evil designs.'

'What else were we supposed to do?' she demanded. 'We couldn't very well chase him into the forest. He came here and we had to put him up.'

'And why did he come here?' he retorted triumphantly.

'Because of your father's advertisement, wantonly offering his chromium pride and joy, his Hillview-born, American-plated gadget. That's why the Yankee came here also. That's why we are swimming in sin and soaked in disaster.'

Her eyes hardened. 'I think you're being simply disgusting. And you aren't even following your own logic. Neither of them was answering the advertisement. One came here on a government mission and the other because he had heard that the mangoes were magical.'

'If your father had done his duty and looked after the health of the village we would not have heard of Hamilton Jones and his orgies. And if he had educated the people as he should have, they would have paid no attention to superstitious nonsense. Clearly and finally, your father is to blame. It is he who plunges the village into this annual stupor of imbecility, where it is prepared to do anything no matter how idiotic: putting up *pandals* which are deliberately designed to fall down, clearing land which is purposely allowed to go to waste so that it can be cleared again uselessly next summer. It's all done to drive us out of our senses, to reduce us methodically into a village of half-wits. Without your father's evil activities this disastrous adventure would never have taken place. If he objected to seizing the mangoes it was only because he had already sown their seeds. He is a creator of the mango mentality.'

'I'm sick of your raving,' Nalini burst out, angrily. 'I came only because I was sorry and wanted to help. But I'm not going to stand here and put up with your rabid insults.'

'None of us is requesting you to stand here.'

Nalini's face crimsoned. Her eyes went round the unyielding circle of faces till they came to where Guruswami's wife sat, her hands stroking her husband's forehead in a monotonous, imploring rhythm of consolation, her look forsaken, piteous and condemning.

'I shan't stay if I'm not needed,' Nalini said.

In her opponent's eyes there was no flicker of interest. 'As you please,' she said, tonelessly. 'It is for the daughter of the master to do as she pleases. I have nothing more to add. The gods have been provoked enough in one day.'

There was nothing more Nalini could do. She went back to the house, hobbling painfully up the path, large portions of which had been wrenched away by the downpour. The rain slapped at her face and the sheet lightning blazed in the sky. It seemed so long since she had come to Mudalur, so long since she had sung that song and the immemorial words had settled round her, binding her to the landscape and its peace. It was so far from yesterday, from the security of the forest, from the deep satisfaction of belonging to the place, of sensing it flow into her, of seeing and shaping whatever lay beyond it, of never needing to retreat into her memories. It was so different now and the skies so full of anger. Yet she could not really believe in what the wind shouted. It was tolerance and gentleness which were real in the cup of the hills. Mudalur was a place where a man could find the essence of his queerness, where life wasn't a constant struggle to maintain a respectable distance from one's self, where people did as they dreamed and let the stars forgive them. The bitterness was there only to pass, a wall that the storm would blow down, a deformity of pain in familiar faces.

She told her father what had happened. He didn't share

the confidence which she felt, perhaps irrationally.

'It's my thirty-second summer here,' he said. 'I suppose it's too long an innings. Well, nobody can say that I didn't have fun.'

'It isn't over yet, Father.' She meant the words, but, standing alone in the night, they sounded helpless.

He patted her head. 'It's a messy homecoming, Nalini. I could have arranged it better. Lakshmi will tell you how for the rest of her life.'

'I never wanted to come back to any other place.'

'Madura and Trichy are much more civilised. We could have made a sensible match there. But I wanted you married in Mudalur. I can't explain it and you won't understand it. Lakshmi quite rightly thinks I was insane.'

'But I *do* understand, Father.'

His voice sounded surprised. 'I'd like to think you really mean that. Unfortunately, I can't tell by looking into your eyes. Indian girls have eyes that are always rinsed with innocence.'

'I feel as you do, Father. You and I have been eating the same mango.'

'I shouldn't have thought so,' he said. 'You're twenty-four years on the wrong side of my fence. I've brought you up and polished you and trained you and heaven only knows what difference it all makes. I know everything that has happened to you, naturally. But I sometimes wonder if I know you at all.'

'Not very well, Father,' she said. 'You can't predict me any more than Mudalur.'

He patted her head again. 'Good night, my child. It is

good to know that happiness can come out of my ignorance. If I lose one world I can always discover another.'

VIII

That night no one slept easily. The wind moaned and writhed around the sandalwood house. The lightning burst out as if consuming the hills. On the concentric zinc roofs of the verandas the rain drummed bellicosely like an endless army of schoolboys. The ground everywhere was sodden as mango pulp.

At four o'clock in the morning Lakshmi arose to prepare breakfast for the members of the doomed mansion. She wasn't the first one up. Sambasivan was already dressed in his ceremonial clothes, rubbing his eyes and despondently flourishing his mace. Ernest was scraping the mud off his puttees.

'Where d'you suppose you've been?' Lakshmi asked Ernest.

'Stashing away the D.D.T. in the forest.'

'Fat lot of good that is. If you've got any spare time you might use it more intelligently. Try to think of some way of getting us out of this mess.'

'I sneaked into the village, too,' said Ernest. 'I figured if we kidnapped Raman they couldn't do anything to us. But they must have figured it also. They've got him guarded like he was the Kohinoor diamond.'

Sambasivan gave his mace a final twist of frustration. 'I feel insecure with this. I think I'd better get my rifle.'

He rummaged in the almirah and excavated a fearsome-looking gadget. Ernest stared at it open-mouthed.

'I've never seen anything like it. Did you put it together yourself?'

Sambasivan beamed. 'How perceptive of you to infer that. It's another one of my multi-purpose projects. The barrel can be attached to a vacuum-cleaner; and with slight modifications it can play atonal music.'

'But can you shoot anything with it?'

'That is a function of minor importance. The apparatus was designed for use during drill with the University Training Corps. I was a colonel in the U.T.C. you know.'

A sigh of despair seeped into the steam of the coffee. They looked towards the door. It was Kubera. The smell of breakfast had awakened him but now that he was awake he could no longer bear the thought of it.

'Sit down,' said Lakshmi. 'It's a very long ascent to the hereafter. One might as well begin it on a full stomach.'

'What do you think they will do to us?' Kubera moaned.

'I really couldn't say,' said Sambasivan. 'But they can't fry us in butter since there isn't any left.'

Kubera wrung his hands. 'Do something. Assert your authority. Offer that bloodthirsty barber a fifty per cent share in my enterprises.'

'Come, come,' said Sambasivan. 'You're the financier type. Surely you've mastered crises like these before? Have you never had angry mobs bashing at your windows?'

'I usually climb into a chartered aeroplane.'

Ernest scowled penetratingly into the mist. 'They're coming,' he said, gulping his coffee down. 'Tell them to take it easy. I haven't been able to load my camera yet.'

The figures began to assemble in the ashen light of the

morning. The mists magnified and multiplied them so that the two hundred and ninety-nine seemed an army of two thousand. They advanced to the house irresolutely, as if there was no other way out. They were not fanatical but simply tired and trod upon. There had been no miracles so they were obliged to build a bonfire.

A more decisive person might have restored the crowd to its natural feeling for order, brought out its latent reluctance to destroy. But Sambasivan appeared portly and incongruous in his ceremonial dhoti with his U.T.C. armament clutched in his left hand and a ladies' umbrella nervously raised in his right. A hoot of derision greeted him. He recoiled from it as from a blow in the face.

'What have you come for?' he demanded, sadly.

'You are old,' Raman said. 'It is natural that you should ask ridiculous questions. We have come to dispose of you and of those whose sins you have sheltered. We have come to cleanse Mudalur of your memory.'

'But why?'

'Because you have ruined us.'

'But how?'

'It is unnecessary to underline the obvious.'

'Sahib,' an underlining voice said from the back, 'our situation is desperate. We are cut off from everyone else. There is sickness in the village. The rain falls unceasingly. Our food has been destroyed and we are starving.'

'That's the unvarnished truth.'

'Disgraceful exploitation.'

'Somebody ought to hang for it.'

'But I had nothing to do with it.'

'Nothing, he says. What about the mango-gatherer?'

'And the Flit-fiend who sprays everything with indecency?'

'But they're only my guests and I didn't even invite them.'

'Didn't invite them, eh? That's adding discourtesy to your other vices.'

'He's guilty,' Raman cried. 'A host is patron to the sins of his visitors.'

'The house is a cesspool of evil.'

'Orgies in there and blasphemy up on the mountain.'

Sambasivan had dropped his rifle. He opened his umbrella in an effort to ward off the storm. 'I can't understand it,' he said. 'Summer after summer I've come back to help you. All that I am is bound up in this village. How can you turn against me? How can two days make nonsense of thirty-two years?'

'Sahib,' a voice said, 'it is as you say: you have been a father to us. When all goes wrong who else is there to blame?'

'Will you surrender quietly?' Raman asked.

Nalini pushed her way to the front. 'Leave my poor father alone, you wretched people.'

'Don't want your fun to be ended, eh!'

'I'm not going to argue,' she said. 'While the discussion has been going on I've been boiling a large urn of Kubera's cosmic tonic. The first man across the threshold is going to get served in the face.'

Raman glared. 'I'll hold you responsible for any violence.'

'I've got something special on the stove for you,' she said. 'It's the hydrochloric acid in which Daddy pickles his cobras.'

'Seize her!' shouted Raman. The crowd hesitated. Mur-

murs of uncertainty began to rise among them. Nalini
watched their indecision and inwardly sighed with relief.

'Are you going to let yourself be bullied by a woman?'

Their faces set. They began to edge forward with un-
nerving slowness. Nalini moved gradually back trying to
fight down the mounting sense of panic, hoping that the
terror hammering at her heart wasn't beginning to show in
her eyes.

She wasn't put to the test. Satyamurti hurled himself
through the doorway and under the noses of the astonished
villagers. His spectacles were drenched with the rain. He
stuck his chin out in order to see more clearly and frowned
reprovingly at the commotion in front of him.

'What is justification for unseemly disturbance?'

'Stay out of this,' Raman said. 'We have an account to
settle with your host.'

Satyamurti put his hand to his left ear and turned it
laboriously in the direction of the voice. 'As I suspected,' he
announced in the other direction, 'village barber is at bottom
of this froth.'

'Don't strain our patience,' Raman said. 'The people here
are determined to have justice.'

'In that case please put to vote proposal that they hang
you.'

'Enough of this!' Raman burst out. 'Stand aside, or take
the consequences.'

'Regret very much I am unable to budge. I am man without possessions or testimonials. Yet owner of house has given
me hospitality. Minimum I can do in return is to prevent
unauthorised entry by hooligans.'

'In that case your blood be on your own thick head, you idiot.'

Satyamurti thrust his nose in Raman's direction, measured him against it and found him sadly wanting.

'Kindly cease anaemic blathering about blood. World knows you are unable to wring neck even of chicken.'

'You'll pay for this,' Raman yelled, his face livid.

Satyamurti pulled out of his shirt pocket a handkerchief somewhat larger than his shirt. He blew his nose ceremoniously. Then before his audience could react he had seated himself immediately in front of the doorway, crossed his legs and put his hands together in an attitude of prayer.

'Ignore him!' Raman cried. 'Let's do our duty and burn down this house. Trample the fool into the ground if necessary.'

'Be careful,' Nalini warned them. 'You've annoyed one *rishi* already. Think again before you murder another.'

Satyamurti's glasses were off his face. He stared myopically at the surrounding menaces. A forest of legs and arms churned and blurred around him. Mud spattered on to his shirt. A hand gripped his shoulder, painfully. He tensed without realising it and then controlling himself made himself limp to the anger of the other man. He stared ahead trying to wipe them out of his vision, compelling himself to see nothing between himself and the emptiness. But he could feel the club poised above him. His scalp prickled and the sweat formed between his clasped hands. He bit on his tongue to prevent himself from crying out and clenched himself round his fear, thrusting upwards, holding firm against the overwhelming will to shrink away. He knew that he

wasn't responding, wasn't moving. He sensed the club lifting away and fought down the surge of relief. Whatever
they did he must not let it affect him. He stared forward
unrelentingly into the hill of his hands.

'Leave him alone,' he was aware of somebody saying.
'Let's see how long he can keep this sham up.'

They trickled down the hill. He could hear Raman pro-
testing to no avail. He wanted to stick out his tongue at
them; he was still insufficiently attuned to holiness and to
the endurance test he was apparently expected to survive.
Without the intensity of fear and of the resistance which it
generated he was too easily aware of the puddle in which he
sat, the broken bits of his spectacles and the unworthy
realisation that he had had nothing for breakfast and was
extremely unlikely to have anything for lunch or for dinner.
There was a long day ahead and no obvious way to spend it.
His left toe was already beginning to go to sleep. He
restrained himself from wiggling it and took stock of his
spiritual resources. He mumbled his way through the sacred
texts he knew; his repertoire was limited to five minutes.
Mathematics absorbed him a little longer, but whatever
figures his mind drew seemed only to hem him in, leaving
him exposed even more dismally to the unceasing axiomatic
certainty of the rain. He was not succeeding. He was too
much the victim of his surroundings. He had to do something drastic to retreat into the waterproof regions of his
inmost personality. He closed his eyes till the red darkness
blackened, and tried to imagine the figures of various gods.
He could not keep them still. They dissolved into shapes
that reminded him of Nalini, that danced around her, pushed

his thoughts towards her. He hammered them out of his sight. He tried to people his mind with abstract patterns, but they were unstable, unsettling, continually becoming alive, persistently pulling in the world outside his head. The rain poured on to his head from the zinc gutter at the edge of the roof. A crow perched on his left shoulder. He opened one eye slightly and could see a kite circling, eyeing him as if he were three-quarters dead. He was wet and hungry and miserable, his shoulder was stiff from the shaking and his legs in the puddle were beginning to lose all feeling. If only he could unfurl an umbrella and smoke a cheroot under it for three minutes. His head was beginning to reel. He looked up blindly into the whirlpool of the rain. The grey cone of the sky's immensity leapt upon him. He tasted the blood on his tongue still oozing from where he had bitten it. The emptiness was dead now. He and only he was moving in it, not living but only moving, pedalling along the endless line of the road, the trees always the same, the telegraph poles never changing, perpetually dividing emptiness from emptiness, not wishing, or hoping, or even accepting, but moving on neutrally into a coma of loneliness, unaware of the peace that was fighting its way into him from the indifferent earth and the dispassionate heavens.

When the evening came the children of the village found him still in the pool, rigid and serene, his clasped hands riveted round the core of himself. His eyes looked through them into a different happiness. They played round him unconcerned, as if he had always been part of the landscape. The adults came later, bringing fruit and milk and apologies.

'We have been in error,' Guruswami's cousin said. 'His

face has chided us rightly. But remember that his back is turned towards your house. We must be free from error. You in your turn must be free from suspicion.'

'Meaning precisely what?' asked Lakshmi, impatiently.

'Your house will not be threatened. Your honoured guests can stay as long as they wish. But your daughter must make her choice tomorrow morning.'

Lakshmi threw up her hands. 'It's impossible. It's insulting. I will not tolerate it.' She glared at Satyamurti who was beginning to straighten his cramped limbs. 'You must act at once to prevent this dastardly outrage. Do your duty and get back into that puddle.'

'The sadhu sahib cannot very well object,' said Raman. 'After all, he happens to be one of the suitors.'

Satyamurti edged away unhappily from the door.

'He is your only defence. If he ceases to side with you and you refuse to accept our terms we can destroy this house with a clear conscience.'

'I accept your terms,' Nalini said, throwing her head back.

'Alas, what is to become of us!' Lakshmi wailed. 'What monster or moron is to be inflicted on me as my son-in-law? Our names will be mud in Madura and damnation in Dindigul.'

Raman looked critically at Nalini. 'At least you seem ready to atone for your mistakes. Or is it because you have no choice?'

'You may be sorry for this later,' Nalini said.

'After tomorrow you will be more than sorry.'

She kept together what she could of her composure. 'Amuse yourself. It can't go on much longer. And now that

I've redeemed myself in your perverted eyes, can Mr Jones
and I do what we can to help poor Guruswami?'

'I see no reason why not.'

They went down to the small brick house. This time the
reception was more tolerant. They set Guruswami's broken
leg and dressed and bandaged his crushed hands. He looked
at Ernest silently and pleadingly.

'They'll be all right,' Ernest said. 'You'll be able to go on
earning your living with them.'

'Sahib, I only wish I could repay you.'

'I wasn't expecting anything.'

'If it pleases you, you can wear my top hat.'

'Get well soon,' Nalini said. 'When I'm married I'll need
another two circles for Hillview.'

'For your sake I'm sorry I slipped on the hill, memsahib.'

'Don't blame yourself,' she said. 'After all it was really I
who slipped first. And you mustn't look at me pityingly,
like that. Mudalur isn't a place where things get too serious.
What happens here deserves a sensible ending.'

IX

Every dawn brought Lakshmi fresh calamities. She could
not sleep and was afraid to wake up. She tossed and moaned
for the third night in succession, shivering indignantly at
the first tremble of light. It was indeed a terrifying morning.
The skies were cloudless, the grass revoltingly green and
the sun shone demoniacally from the unnatural heavens.

She dressed herself grimly in black, cursing Raman as she
applied her make-up. If her daughter was to suffer a fate

222

probably worse than death she would at least bewail the
proceedings with dignity. She began to regret that yesterday's violence had stopped short of its climax. Hillview was
not the noblest of funeral pyres; but to be burned alive was
better than being gossiped about.

She cooked a breakfast which she could not stomach. She
went through her household tasks, trying to prolong them,
but the minutes slipped by, the temporary protections dissolved and before she knew what was happening she was
beneath the *pandal*, praying fervently for the structure to
collapse. Sambasivan was beside her. His mace and his
durbar manners were gone now. He had tried to force his
features into impassivity but he seemed only to have stunned
them into helplessness as he gazed at the gathering with wilting eyes that were too tired for hatred. Behind them the
people thronged in, aggressively gay, cracking jokes in
guilty taste, the more obnoxious among them laying wagers.
To Lakshmi it seemed a bizarre combination of a carnival
and funeral. She looked at the suitors dressed in salacious
white, their eyes aflame with vicious expectations, each one
appallingly more repulsive than the last. She shuddered
wanly and clutched her husband's hands. Whatever the
choice, the result could be only disaster.

There was a hush in the gathering, as Nalini entered.
According to the poet Visvakarman, who in his opinion
immortalised the incident, she was dressed in turquoise,
aquamarine and celestial blue. Her face was serene with
innocence. Her eyes shone with a dignity no humiliation
could debase. So radiant was her loveliness that the sins of
those who had put her on trial fell fainting before her and

were dissolved by her purity. She floated rather than walked; the earth sprang into flower at the caress of her sandals. It is difficult to accept all of Visvakarman's account and one is obliged to sympathise with those critics who complain that he was imposing style upon reality; but if, as is generally believed, he was drunk at the time, it must have been partially with the beauty of his subject since prohibition put no end to his metaphors. In any case, whatever Nalini was wearing, the consensus of astonishment was that she was supremely herself in it, demurely and vividly self-possessed. She entered the situation with a transforming and modest confidence, not as if she owned it, but rather as if she belonged to it. The ribaldry stopped; the sense of guilt was soothed away; everybody had that feeling of contentment which comes only after eating the finest of mangoes. She looked at the wondering, hang-dog faces, her father slumped in dejection, her mother poised as if to upbraid eternity, the five suitors spaced on the way to the fire like milestones on the path to her destruction, and Raman close to the fire itself, his fingers snapping, his eyes absorbing the flames, willing her onwards to her doom exultantly, his razor hovering over the thread of her fate. Then she came forward slowly, her eyes mysterious and mischievous, brimming with a feeling amazingly like happiness, like a child opening the first door to its destiny. She bowed respectfully to her parents, with a vivacious deference that seemed to form again the sense of their dignity and solemnity. She walked past Kalyanasundaram, Satyamurti, Visvakarman and Kubera. There was no hesitation in her steps or in her eyes. She walked serenely past Ernest, who stood looking

at her dumbfounded, too thunderstruck even to aim his
movie camera. She reached the edge of the fire where
Raman stood. The corners of her mouth turned gently upwards. With a humble bow and an expression of impish
solicitude she hung the garland carefully round his neck.

There was a long moment of delighted silence, broken by
the thud of a falling body. It was Lakshmi fainting as a
matter of principle. Raman's eyes darted from corner to
corner helplessly. He squirmed in the garland as if it were
a noose.

'I've been framed,' he yelled. 'Take this infernal thing
off.'

He tried to fling it away. Exultant hands forced it back
upon his shoulders.

'Serve you right, young Raman.'

'Stewed in your own juice, eh!'

'It's about time he got shaved with his razor.'

'My precious,' Nalini said. 'It could never have been anyone else. I'll need a lifetime to explain how much I detest
you.'

Raman glared at her furiously. 'Deeds, not words, will be
used to express my disgust.'

'Just as I hoped, my dearest. To put up with you is the
highest form of penance. Think of the merit I'll gain as a
result. Oh, Raman, how can I ever thank you for practically
guaranteeing me saintliness in my next birth?'

'You're beyond salvation,' he said.

'Then let me devote my doomed life to redeeming you.'

'You're morally outrageous.'

'You're magnetically revolting.'

'If you marry me,' he threatened, 'it will only mean the beginning of your problems. You can't go on living your fancy style of life, lording it over a house infested with servants. You'll have to cook meals and draw water from the well.'

She smiled at him inescapably. 'My dear, deluded, insufferable future husband, as usual you've no idea what you're talking about. You haven't been in the land of the idle rich. But I've been there for three years, living recklessly on my poor father's fortune. I've cooked more than a thousand meals. I've stitched and laundered my own clothes. I've scrubbed the floor twice every week. I've put out the garbage. I've even cleaned the toilet. Have you done any of that with your working-class hands?'

He could hear the crowd tittering behind him. He looked down into her laughing face. Under the stars her eyes would be even more beautiful.

'You can't be wholly beyond redemption,' he said. 'After all, you showed that you were not without taste by selecting me.'

'My beloved,' she said, 'it isn't a question of taste. It's the very first lesson I learned at Columbia. If you can't lick 'em, join 'em.'

5

The Mangoes of Mudalur

THE RESIGNATION of the Community Development
Officer was not expected, but consternation did not shake
the capital. One bureaucrat the less would not be missed,
least of all by the impatient ranks below him. The Branch
Superintendent, who was next in the line of succession,
blessed the day and thought happily of the apple-green sari
which he had so far been unable to afford for his wife. He
glanced at the C.D.O.'s letter without interest and side-lined
the last paragraph. The conclusions were all that really
mattered; the reasoning could safely and justly be ignored.
The man had been successful in his efficiency tests; his future
was assured, his increments certain, his position on the
seniority escalator guaranteed. He had only to stand still to
become steadily more important. If he chose to leave now
it must be because his wits had left him. Or perhaps he had
something to hide. In either case, the steel frame would be
firmer without his support.

He chucked the file into the out-tray at three-thirty. On
second thoughts he attached a priority label to it, not because the case really deserved it, but because delay might

mean that the green sari would be sold. Then he settled down to rewrite his note on centralisation – several changes in it were necessary now that he himself was likely to work in the field.

The Deputy Secretary received the file at ten minutes to six, along with fourteen others sent up to remind him that the Under-Secretary was a man devoted to his work to whom nominal times of office closure meant nothing. He tackled the four *Most Immediates;* they took him all of thirty-five minutes and reduced the stack by only two-thirds of an inch. It was time to go home, but there were relatives in the house and he preferred the tranquillity of the office with the moral effect that working late created. A file did not answer back except when the Joint Secretary read it.

He took the fattest of the priority files. Both the Superintendent and the Under-Secretary had written 'As Proposed' upon it, and with everyone in agreement on whatever it was he could have saved time by applying his own dhobi mark. But the case seemed to have some abnormal features. To begin with the letter was no less than thirty-eight pages. Then, instead of being a recital of the officer's grievances, it was an account of the situation in an obscure village on which the report was only due two months later, and due, moreover, from another officer. Finally, the last sentence excited his curiosity. Obviously those who marked it had not read it. A civil servant did not resign merely because of a desire for redeeming others.

So he began methodically, at the beginning. Mudalur, the C.D.O. had said, was by no means an example for the rest of India; indeed if the anarchy which was alleged to express its peculiar character were to be applied on a nation-wide scale, it would lead to absurdity both comic and disastrous. Even on their own terms developments in Mudalur could not but give rise to grave misgivings. Unless extravagances were gloried in and pressed to eccentric limits. Necessary improvements which the community could well afford were set aside or unreasonably delayed. What logic, for example, was there in an Indian village regularly celebrating the Fourth of July with fireworks? Of course ideal administration was hardly to be expected from the young, ex-Columbia graduate who ruled over the community – and 'ruled' was the right word since the villagers adopted with enthusiasm any proposal of hers, no matter how hare-brained it was shown to be in the cold light of rural economics. Her hold on the inhabitants was difficult to understand since, though brown-eyed, black-haired, translucent-skinned, and moderately beautiful, she was in these respects not noticeably superior to thousands of Indian women who were household oaths instead of local legends. The only obvious difference was in her American education, to which it seemed heretical to attribute her success.

Some time ago, a historic event had taken place in Mudalur, the truth of which could not be ascertained since the mere mention of it caused uncontrollable amusement. As a result, Nalini had married the village barber. The choice was inexplicable and should have been calamitous; but thanks to the lady's golden touch it had, on the contrary, become the cornerstone of the prosperity of the village. Under her guidance her husband had abandoned his profession and turned to another which made striking use of his bizarre but undeniable talents. He was now a professional nose-driller and ear-piercer, armed with a panoply of gold-plated, jewelled-handled instruments lovingly housed in monogrammed, velvet-lined cases, whose reputation was such as to produce ecstatic horror in the most exclusive of families. His dark good looks and faintly diabolical bearing intensified the passionate and mounting demand for his services. To these external qualifications he added an inner genius. He was able to make his operations virtually pain-less. Bloodthirsty though his preparations were, they always dissolved at their climax in a ravishing and unfailing delicacy of touch. It was little wonder that his fame had spread like wildfire. Indeed, few women in India could honestly say that it was not among their secret ambitions to be punctured by Raman on the night of the full moon.

Such popularity unfortunately had its dangerous side. Pierced ears were particularly susceptible to propaganda; wherever Raman went he contrived to leave behind one or more of his subversive leaflets. In the state of serene hypnosis which followed upon a brilliantly successful drilling the most violent incitements seemed like innocuous lullabies. Everywhere Raman's message was being avidly absorbed and enthusiastically propagated. The consequences were limitless. There was no question that the lady from Columbia had devised a political tool of staggering potency. Half the population of India consisted of women and ninety-eight per cent of them had their noses drilled or ears pierced. Immediate and drastic action was essential if Congress was not to lose its hold on the masses. A complete and loyal cadre of drillers and piercers of Raman's quality must be recruited at once. Next year would definitely be too late and Raman might only come to terms if he were given a cabinet portfolio, as Minister of Ears and Noses.

With the output of seditious literature mushrooming, a linotype machine had become economic in Mudalur. One of the ironies of the situation was that this made it possible for the village to publish a considerable amount of criticism and poetry. Perhaps it was unfortunate that most of what was printed should be devoted to the output of a man who was determined to rewrite all that had ever been written so that anyone could read everything simply by buying his works. But Visvakarman's position had its merits, since apart from conserving valuable foreign exchange it also made India culturally self-sufficient.

Mudalur indeed was in what might be called a state of cultural ferment, though it was with some hesitation that he used this worthy phrase to dignify the community's weird activities. At the Institute of Social Involvement, evening lectures were given on such subjects as 'The Arranged Marriage' and 'The Methodology of Deficit Financing', which were attended surprisingly by a large and receptive audience. What distressed the C.D.O. was that in the Institute of Social Renunciation on the other side of the street, in a mango grove, meditations conducted by an extremely holy man with a remarkably long nose were attended enthusiastically by exactly the same people.

The truth was that consistency was not one of the features of Mudalur and that this sad state of affairs, instead of being regretted, was exultantly and even hilariously proclaimed. Approximately three bottles of perfume were consumed every year in the village; yet a factory had been established to produce a new concoction theatrically called Attar of Darkness. On the other hand, the soil was ideal for mangoes; a valuable trade with other areas could have been developed, but production was deliberately inexplicably limited to what the inhabitants were capable of eating. With the prosperity of the village certain to endure since it was built firmly on its seditiousness, one might have expected a far-sighted housing programme that made full use of the natural beauty of the place; yet all plans of this kind had been set at nought by the obstinacy of the villagers, who insisted on living in senseless circular structures to which additional circles were untidily added. To climax everything a quite satisfactory B-class road had been built between the village and Arkayam railway station; but the bridge across a ravine seven hundred feet deep, without which the road was clearly useless, was kept deliberately in a state of disrepair and was in imminent danger of collapsing every monsoon.

When these absurdities were mentioned to the people of Mudalur they nodded sagely instead of providing a sensible explanation, and suggested that all would seem well if a few more mangoes were eaten or if one looked long enough into the eyes of the lady who presided over the fortunes of the place. This was hardly a course of action which a government servant could be expected to consider. Yet it was seriously claimed that it led to enlightenment, merely because those who took the treatment had not so far complained of the consequences and because those who stayed in Mudalur for five days usually stayed on for ever to nod their heads inanely at visitors who asked questions.

By now it should be clear, whatever initial euphemisms had been used in the report, that the experience of Mudalur was indeed a shocking revelation. Here was a place, prosperous without even a plan for survival, flourishing upon its own perversity, wantonly throwing away its windfall advantages, with a population incapable of straightforward thought and ruled erratically by feminine caprices. It was no argument to say that people were themselves in such a place, since every citizen of India knew that the world consisted of programmes, not of people. If he, the C.D.O., proposed to incarcerate himself in such an outpost of lunacy it was only because the process of corruption had gone too deep to be checked by external advice. One could save Mudalur only by living within it. To this mission he was dedicating what remained of his life. The brilliance of the prospects he was sacrificing showed how real was the danger he was endeavouring to avert. It was too much to hope that he would succeed entirely, but he would at least ensure that the example of Mudalur did not spread and that the planned march of progress elsewhere was not impeded by its aberrations. He was leaving to fulfil his mission now. He advised no one to follow him. If he did not emerge after a reasonable interval the bridge over the chasm should be once and for all destroyed.

It was twenty past six. The Deputy Secretary rubbed his chin reflectively. He put the file in his brief-case, went home via the club and borrowed a Raymond Chandler story from the library for the week-end. The tall American at the bar offered him a drink. He sucked in a lime-juice and soda.

'Do you happen to know Mudalur?' he asked.

233

'Do I know it?' echoed Ernest. 'I was the guy who put Muddle Ore on the map.'

'Is it as terrible as they say it is?'

'It's much, much worse,' said Ernest. 'A man can spend all his life there trying to make sense of it. It rains too much and the people are impossible. But the mangoes there taste better than anywhere else.'

The Deputy Secretary smiled and returned the drink. He went home and ate a prosaic dinner. When his relatives were asleep he took the file to his study. His suitcase stood beside the telephone table. With a mild effort, he restrained himself from packing it. He undid the tape and wrote 'As Proposed' below the previous signature. He could have done it four hours ago. Nobody would realise what lay behind the ditto.

At Arkayam station the train stopped, exhausted. One passenger got off. The rain was falling solidly and the skies were the colour of post office ink, but he gave the porter his umbrella as well as his suitcase. With a seraphic smile, he undid his shirt buttons so that he could be more satisfactorily drenched. The man at the soft drink stall watched the performance, tapped his head in commiseration and held out a mango.

The C.D.O.'s face glowed to the extent that the downpour allowed. He seized the fruit and bit passionately into it. It cascaded down his chin and on to his chest. He clapped his hands delightedly, called for the only bullock-cart and looked up into the skies with radiant contentment as the animal's feet turned in the direction of Paradise.

BALACHANDRA RAJAN

Balachandra Rajan was born on 24 March 1920 and educated at Presidency College, Madras, and at Cambridge University. He graduated from Cambridge in 1941 with first-class Honours in Economics and later took first-class Honours in English. In 1944 he became a Fellow in English at Trinity College and in 1946 he received his Ph.D. in English from Cambridge University. He was Director of Studies in English at Trinity College from 1946 to 1948 and in 1947 he lectured in modern poetry at Cambridge University.

Balachandra Rajan joined the Indian Foreign Service in 1948, and after a period of service in the Ministry of External Affairs was assigned to the Permanent Mission of India to the United Nations to which he was an Advisor for seven years. He has represented India on several international bodies such as the United Nations Children's Fund, the Commission on International Commodity Trade and the Preparatory Commission of the International Atomic Energy Agency. He was for two years Chairman of the Executive Board of the Children's Fund and is currently the Representative of India to the International Atomic Energy Agency.

His books include *'Paradise Lost' and the Seventeenth Century Reader, T. S. Eliot: a Study of his Work by Several Hands, Modern American Poetry,* and his first novel, *The Dark Dancer.* He was editor of the English magazine *Focus* and has contributed poetry and criticism to several English and American periodicals.